12-07

Year of the
DOG

Year of the
DOG

A NOVEL

by SHELBY HEARON

UNIVERSITY OF TEXAS PRESS ❧ AUSTIN

James A. Michener Fiction Series, James Magnuson, Editor

The James A. Michener Center for Writers at the University of Texas commissioned the editing and proofreading of this book.

Requests for permission to reproduce material
from this work should be sent to:
    Permissions
    University of Texas Press
    P.O. Box 7819
    Austin, TX 78713-7819
    www.utexas.edu/utpress/about/bpermission.html

The paper used in this book meets the minimum requirements
of ANSI/NISO Z39.48–1992 (R1997) (Permanence of Paper).

Library of Congress Cataloging-in-Publication Data

Hearon, Shelby, 1931-
  Year of the dog / by Shelby Hearon. — 1st ed.
    p.   cm. — (The James A. Michener fiction series)
  ISBN-13: 978-0-292-71469-4 (alk. paper)
  ISBN-10: 0-292-71469-6 (alk. paper)
  1. Guide dogs—Fiction. 2. Burlington (Vt.)—Fiction. I. Title.
  PS3558.E256Y43 2007
  813'.54—dc22   2006022585

With love to Wendy Weil,
a dog person;
with special thanks to Peggy Rush
for all her help;
and in memory of Nexus,
a cherished black lab and
trusty companion.

I'm broken in.
Pack up the dreams and let the life begin.

—C. S. Lewis, *Dymer*

Year of the DOG

Socializing

Puppies with good health and lineage are matched
with waiting raisers who have the love and time
to live with them for a year and help them grow
into confident, serene, and friendly companion dogs.

—*Puppy Manual*

AT FIRST I thought it was great, to meet someone who had no past. We were at the Dog Park, my new puppy and I, at the large spread of hillside on Lake Champlain where everybody let their dogs run loose, a dozen breeds, Labradors, shepherds, akitas, terriers, chasing those watermelon-slice Frisbees in the early twilight.

I had her, Beulah, on the thirty-foot soft leash called the umbilical cord that allowed her to sniff and get acquainted with the big dogs, plus with assorted fragrant car tires, blocks of granite, and scent-marked tree bark. She wasn't really *my* puppy, not for keeps. She was a puppy-in-training to be a companion dog to some blind person. That's what I was doing for a year up here in the state of Vermont, raising this tail-wagging creamy lab for someone else.

I hadn't set out to be somebody who did good for people. In high school, I wanted to run a competitive half-mile; instead I played good-enough basketball, because I was tall, and because Peachland, South Carolina didn't have the least interest in a girls' track team. What happened to change things, was I started working afternoons, part-time, my junior year at the pharmacy, doing whatever Mr. Sturgis, the pharmacist, wanted me to do. And that got me to see that I could do some things for the people who were ill and uncomfortable that he couldn't do.

For instance, when Mr. Grady, an elderly black man with a number of health problems, came in waving a new prescription, I could know that his doctor, Dr. Bayless, totally didn't remember that he gave Grady something last month which was going to mix with this one about the same as giving a hemophiliac a blood thinner or a diabetic on the way to a coma a piece of divinity. This meant I'd need to call the doctor's helper, who wore white like a nurse but wasn't really a nurse, to suggest, "I believe Dr. Bayless is filling a prescription that's maybe not okay. Do you think?" And then I'd hear her tell Bayless, and him say, "Shit," and "Thank the girl," and then heave into a hacking spell of coughing. I could excuse that, knowing also that his own health had taken a turn for the worse. Or when Mrs. Runyan, the mother of the man who owned my daddy's hardware store, came in, leaning on her cane, to pick up some medicine for a bad diagnosis, and looked up at me and whispered, "I never did like gladioli," I could know it meant she was associating the flowers with funerals, and she didn't want one. And tell her not to miss a dose.

So that this spring when Curtis Prentice, my husband of five years, and steady for three more before that, ripped my heart out and stomped on it in front of every single person in town, what tore me up was that by then I'd changed. I wasn't the Janey Daniels I'd been at seventeen when he'd dropped Millie the Cheerleader and started hanging out with me, when being with him, such a hunk, was the total of what I wanted to do; I'd become a woman who'd got some sense and charity. That was what hurt the worst, that he, Curtis, dumped me in full public view when I'd got to be a better person.

And on top of trying to hold my face up in public, in private my folks wanted to talk the mess of my marriage to death. What if I'd taken Curtis's name the way I should have when we married?—that was my mom. What if I'd had myself a baby, being married five years without, that didn't look right.—that was my daddy. But they didn't argue when I told them I had to get out of town, and Mr. Sturgis didn't either, when I asked him for a sabbatical from the pharmacy. Daddy explained to the people who came into the hardware store that his Janey would be going to a cooler climate for a spell to get out of the Carolina heat; Mom told everyone at church that she had blood kin still living in Vermont who would look after her daughter in this trying time. And Mr. Sturgis, who didn't want me gone at all, generously relayed the information that I'd gone north for a spell to study up on new breakthrough drug developments.

Today, realizing my problem wasn't likely to go away with mooning around on an early June afternoon cooler than a winter day at home, I tried to get in a better frame of mind. Zipping up my new red windbreaker against the chill, I led my puppy toward the lake front where I hoped to see ducks upending themselves in the rough windblown water.

It was then I saw this person headed my way. He looked like a college boy, a Vermonter for sure, in heavy boots, shorts, a couple of worn-thin t-shirts, something tied around his forehead, scroungy face-hair. And the nervous way of a lot of boys I'd known in high school. It lifted my spirits just seeing him, the kind of boy I'd had in class but never got to know. The kind who sat in front of you and cracked their knuckles and dug out their ear wax and had to root around in the top of their socks during the teacher's demonstration of the lever and pulley, like they'd lost something down there. Who'd probably moved from somewhere else, and, naturally, aced the Physics final, the Math final, the, even, Social Studies final (because they read the newspaper and had been to Washington twice with their dad, and even knew the current names of the countries in Africa).

The point being I was glad to see him, this sort of guy I hadn't gone out with or even given too much thought to. The type I'd hear in the halls talking to his only buddy about the sort of deep and shallow stuff guys like that talked about: What is the ultimate meaning of our existence, and Do you have a rash on your ankles, or what?

I aimed a smile in his direction and waited, needy for a little conversation with somebody who didn't know a thing about me. After all, I'd driven all the way nearly to Canada to get to some place where the people I met would be strangers. Knowing that if I'd taken an apartment for a year while things cooled down, in Atlanta, say, or Asheville, or even Chattanooga, I'd have run into someone visiting a daughter-in-law or a sick mama, or someone having a reunion with her grade school friends or getting himself a loan at a bigger bank. And they'd have gossiped back home about how I looked, how poor Janey was managing, trying to put a good face on the break-up.

"Hey," the boy said, catching up with me on the path that led to the lake. He had a handsome big furry three-colored dog with him, and seemed to know how to get along with dogs. A good sign.

"Hi," I answered, noticing he didn't seem to mind that I was tall enough to be eye-level with him, which a lot of guys did, wanting you to be someone smaller than them, to come up to their shoulder. I held out a hand. "I'm Janey."

"James." He hesitated. "Martin." He located his hand, stuck it out.

I remembered Mr. Haynes, the elderly man I helped at the pharmacy back home who had a companion he called Blind Dog and how you always had to greet the dog first, and I told him, "This is Beulah," since she was looking up at the new tall person expectantly and wagging her tail.

"Hello, Beulah," he said to her in a nice tone.

"What kind of dog is yours?" I asked, watching as the husky animal which looked like a small St. Bernard snapped at the gusty wind, as if dreaming of the Alps.

"Bernese Mountain dog." He looked a bit sheepish, and fiddled with the thing tied around his forehead. "It's not actually mine. I don't even know his name. I'm walking it for one of my students. I teach high school kids who are part of a study abroad program." He seemed embarrassed. "The kids tell you, *You want to meet someone, get a dog.*"

I smiled in friendly way, to let him know it had worked. He wasn't as young up close as I'd thought. And he had to be already out of school to have students, though he must not have a steady sort of job—to be dressed down like that in the late afternoon on a weekday. "This isn't really my dog either," I told him. "Not exactly." I explained as we walked together to the rocky lakeshore, how I'd have her for a year, get her mannerly and socialized, and then she'd go to the place in Massachusetts where they trained them to be the companions of blind people. I tried to sound confident about that, my looking after her.

The truth was that I hadn't been Beulah's person but a few weeks and still hadn't got used to having something warm and breathing around all the time. I'd never had a dog before. It seemed, growing up, that every kid but me had one, some dog that waited at home and wagged its tail and had to be taken for a run before breakfast or to the playground after school. But my mom wouldn't hear of it, griping that you'd have to clean up their poop, your kitchen would smell of Alpo and your furniture would shed dog hairs. Curtis didn't either for a minute consider us getting a dog. He'd done that once in his life, he said. Who'd bathed the mangy black-and-white mutt at his house? Not anyone else, you could bet on that. Who'd got the ticks off in the sticky, buggy, buzzing summertime, the dumb dog having run into the high weeds on some vacant lot? The son was who, he was who.

Beulah went all around the big dog, wagging her tail in imitation of him, then looking up at me to see if that was all right. I decided that of course it was when she was on the loose

leash, the play-time leash. She let him sniff at her and then
sniffed him, and they ran around and she looked thrilled to be
with another dog so close, and I realized she must miss her litter puppies in her new life.

The teacher and I enjoyed them for a spell while he dug
around in one ear and then tried to scratch an itch in the middle of his back. "I like labs," he said, as Beulah wriggled under
the big mountain dog like he was a step-ladder, her ears brushing his furry stomach. "She four months?" he guessed.

"Three," I told him.

He studied her. "That sounds hard, to raise it and then, uh,
give it away like that."

"I don't know," I admitted. "I haven't done this before. I'm
just—visiting," I said. "I'm taking a sabbatical."

He looked as if that sounded okay. And didn't ask why or
from what, which warmed me to him a lot.

We saw the wind-whipped lake make whitecaps around
two kayakers and a windsurfer, and, far off almost to the New
York shore, watched a pair of sailboats listing sideways. We
talked about the ducks and why there weren't more, since, he
said, they loved choppy water and usually traveled in groups.
And I asked why it was dogs tried to take the wind in their
mouths, the way his did.

After a while, he guessed he'd better return the borrowed
dog to his student, hanging back a few minutes like he wasn't
in a rush, retying a boot lace, standing around long enough for
me to notice blue eyes, which you didn't often see with nearly
black hair. Then the two of them set off at a brisk pace, taking a short-cut across a green field behind the tennis courts.
Watching his back in its faded tees, I had a moment of regret
that when I was young and dumb I'd fallen for a no-good
stud—and let all those fidgety boys go by without giving them
a glance.

2

WHEN I FIRST arrived in May, I'd got totally crazed that I wasn't going to find any place to live, since the occupancy of apartments in Burlington, even with school out, stood at 105 percent the paper said (but surely they knew that couldn't be right). While I was hunting, I'd got myself a motel room, for a cheap weekly rate, south of town, at a place called PACIFIC VIEW. That blew my mind, up here in the Green Mountains on an inland lake, and I sent a postcard home to my folks: *Pacific View, Vermont*. But it turned out the name was because the small service station next door was called Pacific Gas. View of the gas station.

The thing was, the Companion Dog people didn't want your puppy confused at the start of your being together by being in a motel. When you took a puppy to raise, you had to be able to put her crate in the location where it would stay, for when she needed to sleep in the beginning or when you needed to put her up, if you were going out without her. Plus, at the start, you had to take her outside every hour to the same place in the yard, and then you called her name and said, "Get busy;" the first time the puppy peed where she was supposed to, you smothered her in hugs and told her, "Good girl." So naturally they didn't want her starting out in some temporary place, and getting confused by a move to new quarters and a strange yard with no familiar scent.

The rental ads I'd circled—that promised NEAR THE HOSPITAL or CLOSE TO UNIVERSITY, central locations in this town which sprawled along the lake and that seemed safe to me—naturally also said NO SMOKING and NO PETS. A few came right out and said NOT A PARTY HOUSE, which made it clear that the landlords had headaches about property damage and noise from students. So I started driving up and down the hilly streets, writing down every phone number from the cardboard signs stuck in front yards that had no realtor listed. What a discouragement. Half the time they didn't return my call—no surprise, since my cell had a Carolina exchange and who wanted to leave a message for a transient at the PACIFIC VIEW MOTEL? I'd been scouting in a dress and jacket, carrying a notebook, trying to look like a single professional who wouldn't make trouble, but I needn't have bothered. By the time I wheeled back by, the rental sign would already be gone and guys would be unloading boxes, moving in.

But finally my luck changed, and I got a look-see at a place a few blocks from downtown in a decent area with rentals and owner-homes scattered together. Seeing a short, scowling, portly man hammering a sign into a grassy front yard, I screeched to a halt on a steep street that plunged west toward the lake. From the outside, the place looked too good to afford—a narrow red-brick house, at least a century old, with a high front porch up half a dozen steps. Braking and leaping from the car, I hustled over to him. Looking down on his combed-over hair, I inquired in my most professional voice about an apartment, at which the man dropped his hammer and grudgingly admitted, "I got one vacancy."

Inside the front door, I stopped dead still. We stood crammed in a dark closet-like entry with three doors, the middle one apparently leading upstairs. Walls had been nailed where there hadn't ever been walls. "Somebody sure chopped up this old house," I blurted out, forgetting myself.

The landlord opened the door on the right. "My brother-in-law did the work here," he said, as if to explain. Then, staring at me, he added, "You're from somewhere, aren't you? You got an accent."

"From down South," I admitted, hoping that didn't ruin the deal.

The available apartment, which I followed him into, must have been the original home's parlor, now with a fake fireplace, scuffed wood floors, a ratty maroon sofa and wing chair, a single ceiling light. Entering the large kitchen, however, I got a nice surprise. Light and airy, it had a decent table by a window, and its own back door with steps leading down into a small half-fenced backyard. Just the size for one growing puppy.

"The bedroom?" I asked, back in the living room, looking for an interior hall.

"This is it," the landlord explained, impatient. "This one's the efficiency. In there's the bathroom."

I investigated the not-so-clean facilities and took a deep breath. I didn't really expect a cottage with climbing roses, but I guess I hadn't dealt with what it meant, having both a university and a college in a stone's throw, competing with thousands of students for four walls and running water.

"I'll take it," I said, carefully not mentioning the canine companion I was planning to room with. "If the sofa makes into a bed."

"It's not furnished, what gave you the idea it was furnished?" he hollered out, raising his voice as if anybody who spoke so slow might also be deaf.

"I'll take it if you leave the furniture that's here and put me a lock on the inside door."

"You put it there yourself, Miss. That'll be two months in advance. The furniture'll cost extra."

I wanted to yell at him, Do I look like I'm going to pay that, for half an apartment without a bedroom and a stall for a bath? But he narrowed his eyes like he didn't have all day, and was locking up the look-see by the time I got the check written. I'd just barely moved my savings into a bank on Bank Street (things were so literal up here!), but figured it would clear. He tossed me two keys (front door, back door) and we signed one of those standard leases that must come by the ream from Staples.

And that's how I got a home for Beulah. A home with a grassy backyard bathroom spot for her, under a huge hardwood tree with sweet-smelling white flowers, and, in a neighboring yard, a larger spoor-crazed hardwood raining white lint on the lawn. At that time, early June, with a perfumed breeze and an almost warming sun, I didn't of course foresee the matter of the Vermont winter.

———

The day my puppy was to be brought to me, I got up at sunrise, now five o'clock in the morning here in the north. Too psyched to sleep any longer on the lumpy ancient hideaway bed. I'd never spent all my time before with another living being, and it made me slightly panicked. You'd think marriage would be like that, but if you've been married you know that it isn't. You are at work and he is at work, or maybe he's off with his buddies and you're looking at the Carolina summertime grass, wondering if you need to water or if the ragged remnants of some early tropical storm is going to do the job for you. You're together at night—having supper, then he's trying to make a deal and you're talking to your mom, then you're in bed and things are going smooth or they're going rocky, then it's morning and your head is on your work. But here I'd signed up for someone who I was going to have to keep with me all the time, hearing her noises, feeling her nose against my leg, rushing out the back door to take her down the open wooden stairs, brushing her soft pale coat and checking her ears, teaching her to listen for her name.

I broke out in a cold sweat. Terrified at the idea of having someone else breathing in the same room with me night and day, I went down into the yard, barefoot, in the oversize t-shirt I slept in, figuring no one else would be awake, and stood under the tree. Practicing aloud, along with the early birds, "Get busy," "Good dog," "Good girl."

But when the Companion Dog lady knocked on my door hours later and the creamy little lab trotted inside, looking all around the strange room as if to say, "*Where is my person, where is my person?*" I forgot about my nerves. Getting down on my hands and knees, twenty-five-years old and never had a dog, I touched my nose to hers. "Hi," I said, "Hi, Beulah." Because they had already told me her name—explaining that the first letters of the names indicated the order of puppies and the litter from that year. The Companion, a pleasant woman named Betty, who donated her time, gave me the thick puppy manual, with every possible instruction on care and training, and her crate. And then the woman rubbed the puppy's coat, handed me the leash—and left Beulah in my care. We stood looking at each other, her tail wagging, until, after a moment, breathing deeply, I lifted her in my arms and carried her, warm and wiggling and with a clearly beating heart, down the back stairs into her new flower-scented yard.

Now, when we got home from the Dog Park and our meeting with the three-colored mountain dog and his person, she and I descended the open steps, and while she got busy, I stood thinking of what it might be nice to have for supper. I was missing southern food and wishing that instead of filling her water bowl and pouring out her chow, I could let her share my meal and then lick my plate, as I imagined ordinary dogs got to do.

3

MOM AND DADDY were the kind who kept up with anybody the least bit kin to anybody they knew in any way. Whenever I stopped by their house back home, I could count on hearing them catching up with the latest on some one of Mother's friend Madge's Alabama cousins, or the brand new wife of the oldest son of the man who owned Daddy's hardware. So, naturally, because of this outlook, they'd assumed that the minute I got to Vermont my mom's only living blood relative, her maternal aunt, Mayfield Mason, would be having me to supper all the time and doing my laundry, that she'd be finding me a mechanic and a medical doctor, that she'd call every day and want to take me shopping. But the truth was, I'd been in town over a month and hadn't heard a word from her.

It became clear to me that I was going to have to be the one to call on her, being the new person in town with time to spare, and realizing that there was no way the older woman would understand why I was using up my entire life savings to spend a year where I didn't know a soul. Getting up my resolve the day after Beulah and I went on our outing to the Dog Park, I set out to find her house. Not thinking to phone ahead to ask when it might be convenient for me to drop by, not picking up some nice gift to present her with or even bringing a batch of homemade buttermilk biscuits to remind her of where she came from. Just tired of hearing Mom's constant reminders that this aunt was the excuse she'd given everyone about why I'd picked Vermont for my sabbatical.

While I dried my hair and my puppy had her breakfast, I reread the letter Mom wrote her aunt, and then the one she received in return—after having waited on pins and needles for a two full weeks.

———

Dear Aunt May,

This is your only niece writing to you, to let you know that my daughter Janey will be visiting in your town for the year, seeing another part of the country and doing a little charity work involving dogs for blind people. I hope this letter paves the way for you to take an interest in her being in Burlington.

I don't know if you recall that she was until recently married to the Prentice boy, but since she did not take his name at the time, she'll be going by Daniels. That may have been part of the problem, but who am I to say?

While I am writing, I also want to thank you again for your good words and the generous spray of flowers when my mama, your sister, passed away. She was sorry to be out of touch with you.

Thanks in advance from your only niece,
Ida Jean Daniels

P.S. Also I want to say I hope that Janey can meet your good friend Bert Greenwood, all of whose murder mysteries I personally have read.

———

Dear Ida Jean,

What a surprise to hear from you, as I have quite lost touch with the family in recent years. Certainly, I will be glad to help Janey get settled as best I can, although I can't imagine a capable young person her age having much need of the advice or company of a semi-retired librarian.

With best wishes to you
and Talbot,
Aunt May

———

It took me a while to locate her house at the corner of Larch and Gum, at the end of a street with two fenced cemeteries, around the corner from a synagogue and a Quaker meeting house, since most of the streets in town were named for trees, and twice I turned the wrong way and found myself back by the university and the hospital.

I pulled up on the grass of a deep lot, in front of a two-story brick house shaded by the same dark-barked tree with fragrant white blooms that sheltered Beulah's bathroom. Locking her in the car, I told her to stay, gently pushing her down on the floor of the front seat where Companion Dogs were supposed to ride, and left the window cracked open wide enough for her to get a scent of the flowering trees. Would that be confusing?

The woman at the door stood uncertainly, staring at me. My height, she had gray-brown hair with bangs, glasses, and wore loose jeans and old tennis shoes. "Yes?" she inquired, not unfriendly in her tone.

"I'm Janey—." I faltered. "Your niece? Ida Jean's girl? I should have phoned to give you some warning. I was just out for a drive and I thought——." I blushed or at least my face got hot. "I guess since I've been up north here I've forgotten my manners."

"Come in, won't you?" The woman, who had to be Aunt May, studied me a minute, then stepped aside. "You've caught me in dungarees and sneakers, I'm afraid," she said. She found us chairs in a room with old furniture and walls of books. "Did she write me you were coming, your mother? I'm sure she did." She sighed and put her glasses on her head. "Are you getting settled then, here in Vermont?"

I nodded. "I guess I thought you'd look like my grandmama. I mean not *like* Grandmama, but——." I didn't know how to say she didn't look like family, and I'd expected that she would, that she'd be someone if I'd passed her on the street I'd have known she belonged to us.

She considered. "You have my height," she said. "My father, your great-grandfather, was a tall man. Though you have the hazel eyes and fair hair of my mother's side." Then she rose, as if we'd got too personal. "I was making tea. Will you drink it hot?"

I told her yes, taking it as a good sign that she remembered that *iced* tea, usually sweetened to the gills, was the Carolina state drink. I fretted that maybe I shouldn't have said what I did, remembering that Grandmama had got her nose out of joint about her sister who'd left the state and gone off to Vassar College and had never made a family of her own or kept up with the one God gave her. She used to say that May had been serious about someone while still a girl, but her dad put an end to it. In recent years, Mom got a thrill out of hearing that Aunt May had got herself a boyfriend, at her age, the Vermont mystery writer named Bert Greenwood, which put her somewhat back in favor with the family. Though we didn't hear about it till the week of Grandmama's funeral.

Looking around the large room, I wondered how it would

be to end up like this great-aunt, in your seventies in a north-
ern climate between two mountain ranges, living alone.
Librarians, like pharmacists, maybe, must be people who
helped you out when you weren't sure what to ask for or what
to do with it when you got it. But was that enough?

When Aunt May came back with two cups on a tray, I
mentioned that I had my puppy-in-training in the car. "I think
my mom wrote you I was raising one? I wonder, could I bring
her in?"

The tall woman in jeans looked out the wide bay window.
"The dog. Yes, I believe Ida Jean did mention that. Perhaps—."
She clasped her large hands together. "Perhaps another time."

We had bitter brewed tea and I didn't ask for lemon or use
the cream but drank it straight, nearly the color of coffee. I
talked about how early it grew light in the mornings this far
north, and how late it stayed light in the evenings. How the
summer days were so amazingly long I found myself wanting
to take a dawn run along the lake or a late-night walk downtown. "Is it hard in the winter? Having it the other way?"

"I've grown to like the contrast." She sipped her tea.

"I never had a dog before," I told her, my mind on wishing
I'd come dressed in something better than shorts and a tee, my
hair just-washed and flying in all directions. "She's just a
puppy—."

"All dogs were once puppies," she commented dryly.

Silenced by her tone, I wondered what else I could talk
about, if she had an interest in hearing what Mom was doing
in Peachland or what in a general way was going on these days
in our upland part of the state.

But then Aunt May asked a nice question, as if she realized
she'd sort of shut me up. "What made you decide to raise a
dog during your year here, Janey?"

And, grateful she'd asked about that instead of prying into
the business of my splitting with Curtis, I told her the whole

story about Mr. Haynes, the blind man who came into the pharmacy all the time because he couldn't remember which shaped pill was for what ailment and needed reminding. How he always brought his guide with him, the big black lab he called Blind Dog. How I asked him about where had he got the dog and how did they place them with a blind person. And that he'd told me a great lady over in Greenville had raised the dog so it knew just what to do from day one, so he didn't have to use his blind stick anymore. "I thought about that, because I saw him a lot and had grown fond of Blind Dog who always came in with him. And I figured if I was going to come way up here, and not have my work at the pharmacy for a spell— well, I wanted to at least be doing something for somebody."

"As I recall," Aunt May said, "the Haynes family is black. Is that correct?"

"Yes, ma'am, he is. And so is his dog." And I laughed out loud, I couldn't help myself, it was a southern joke.

She smiled. "I haven't heard the sound of Carolina for years." Then, setting down her teacup, she took off her glasses to clean them, and that seemed a signal it was time to go.

Outside, after glancing quickly toward the car to make sure Beulah hadn't climbed up on the seat (the way a child or an ordinary dog would), I asked my great Aunt May the name of the towering tree with the rough bark and scented white flowers that I'd been living with but didn't know.

"That's a black locust." She seemed pleased I'd asked. "I like them a lot." She gestured behind her. "These three are older than the house." She stopped to pick a twig off the ground. "Perhaps you would like a tree book, Janey. Would you? I have a slew. Librarians seem to accumulate a world of reference books."

"I would," I said. And, waiting in the windy air for her to bring it, felt grateful that now I'd have something to tell them at home about my visit to Mom's remaining blood kin.

4

AFTER SUPPER, I dug my cell out of my tote bag and called Mom and Daddy. It was no secret they still had mixed feelings about my coming up here. Mom pretended to be chipper about it, how I needed to get away for a spell, but she kept on telling me all the gossip just as if I'd never left, not getting the idea that the whole reason I'd come up here was to get away from everybody like her minding everybody else's business.

Daddy couldn't help being of two minds. On the one hand, he wanted what was best for his girl, on the other he didn't warm to the idea of sending me off to a state which had just that spring declared civil unions legal. Whatever racism he'd inherited from his daddy had been rubbed away after thirty years of working at the hardware store, where, he liked to say, you could see who was doing the hard work and who wasn't, and who built straight and who built crooked. But he still had a blind eye in the direction of people loving their own kind. "You watch out," he'd said when I was packed and the car loaded for the drive, "up there anybody can marry anybody."

"I went to see Aunt May," I told them. "She served hot tea, and gave me a book on trees."

"That's her being a librarian," Mom explained.

"What? Her heating up the tea?" Daddy interrupted.

I said, "I'm not sure she remembered that I was supposed to be up here—she seemed surprised to see me."

"Now don't you go casting a stone about the treatment you got, hear? So many different apples fell off our family tree we could change our name to Newton. She'll look after you."

"She didn't like the idea of me bringing the puppy inside."

"Well, of course," Mom nearly shouted, "she doesn't want to have a *dog* in her house. Didn't you listen to what I told you? Didn't you read Bert Greenwood's books which I sent you up there with two of? Those mysteries, every single one, has some kind of bad-dog event in the past of somebody, somebody deceased or maybe the suspect, and this judge always has to retire to his chambers to get over hearing about it, before solving the case. He sometimes has to have a glass of bourbon, and your daddy, who is on the other line listening in, says to ask you, Do they drink bourbon up there in Vermont, he thinks it's only in the South."

I hadn't read the books, which probably were still in the unpacked box in the trunk of the car. I remembered they were all set in a little town in Vermont, spelled like CHARlotte, the town in North Carolina, but pronounced CharLOTTE. They all had titles which sounded like something you'd heard before, which I guess was the point: *Charlotte's Web, Charlotte Ruse, The Prisoner of Charlotte.* But if Bert Greenwood or anybody was living with Aunt May, I didn't have an inkling of it.

I had to admit to Mom that I hadn't got around to reading the mysteries yet, but promised her I would soon. "I've been spending all my time with Beulah," I explained, and patted my trusty puppy who, hearing her name, had padded over to stand beside me. Good girl.

"Beulah?" Daddy's voice broke in.

"The *dog*, Talbot," she said. "The dog." Then, just when she'd shooed him off the line and I thought the call was over, Mom added in a whisper: "Hon, there's some news you might not want to be hearing, so stop me if you're going to get upset."

5

I'D KNOWN MILLIE Dawson longer than I'd known Curtis. She had been a thorn in my side from grammar school through high school. At least that was my side of the story. She'd sat behind me in homeroom, and always had to ask the teacher if she could move in front of me so she could see the board or if I'd just remove my head. She was one of those girls that the rest of us had a jealousy just looking at: a waist about the diameter of my ankle bone, boobs like cup cakes, hair that bounced even when she sat still. Bitsy and limber and energetic, she could do the split and jumping jacks, and made me—a pretty good athlete actually—feel large and lumbering.

She'd been wild in love with Curtis Prentice forever, and when, our senior year, he'd asked me to the senior all-night party instead, I didn't have a guilty minute. I figured she could've had anybody in the state of South Carolina she wanted. I never spent an instant wondering if she cried herself to sleep when he started up with me, or if she ripped out my pictures in the yearbook. Instead, I floated six feet off the ground because I, good serious Janey Daniels, working part-time at the pharmacy after school, had taken Curtis Prentice, hunk, away from Millie Dawson.

All of this I needed to remind myself about, having just heard from the town's biggest rumor-spreader, Mom, that

Millie had already been three months pregnant before I knew she'd stolen my one-time husband back.

Whimpering enough to cause my wagging, padding, pale-faced puppy to settle down at my feet, on her tummy, paws forward, listening for her name, I tried to eat the plate of faux-Caesar salad with chicken I'd put together before the call home. Deciding lettuce didn't do much for a squirrelly stomach, I added a cold bottle of Magic Hat beer.

My brain remembered the thrill of that time, when everything about Curtis had stopped my heart. He'd walk down the street moving fast and smooth, like a halfback about to run for a tackle, eating a cone or a burger with one hand, waving to the town with the other. When he started hanging out with me, he talked a lot about my ambition. He wanted to catch some of it, he said, because he wanted to make something out of himself. So when it became clear I liked my job at the pharmacy and wanted to make that my work, he'd stop by, talking to me about what did I think about the emergency medical service, didn't I think they did more than the doctors?—being right there on the spot when somebody had a heart attack or got themselves in a car accident? He got excited about the EMS, figuring if he worked for them we'd be in the same field: saving lives.

By the time we got our diplomas, he'd begun riding with the ambulance crew, studying up on first-aid measures. And I guess I started to split in two at that time: trying to get my pharmacy degree and trying to hang onto Curtis. It didn't take much persuasion to talk me into a wedding while I was still in school at USC. I guess at that time I'd have followed him nude down the street with a rose in my teeth if he'd asked.

But things worked out differently between me and Curtis from what I'd expected. He gave up on making a living or even getting a lot of satisfaction from riding ambulances. He thought about being a nurse, but his buddies made a lot of jokes about *Nursie Curtis,* and he'd given up on that. His dad suggested he try life insurance: Who helped the injured guy the most? Who helped him in his back pocket? So he did that, became a claims adjuster. That might've been fine, except that people in town kept telling him his wife had sure been a help, how she'd got their husband off his deathbed. People kept asking him, Are you Pharmacist Daniels' husband? And then one day somebody brand new to town hollered out the car window, "Afternoon, Mr. Daniels." And Curtis came home, his face blazing, and shouted at me. "You think you're the tail, don't you, Janey? Well, you're not the tail and you're not gonna be wagging me."

When he took the case for Mr. Dawson, promising to get him a truck-load of money for an injury to his back—some dumb nut hitting his car broadside in a pile-up—he made a trip by the pharmacy to tell me. "I'm gonna get him a bundle. Man just wants to get his car overhauled; I'm gonna get him enough to buy the dealership."

"Is that Millie's daddy?" I'd asked. It came out of my mouth, the wrong question, old people in wheelchairs and a couple of regulars waiting, and me, all of a sudden, acting like I was back at Peachland High.

"If he is, what about it? You don't remember that I haven't been with her since the day I nearly broke my ass trying to hook up with you? You don't remember that? I bet *she* remembers that. You want me to tell him I can't make the deal, it wouldn't be ethical to get him his wad of compensation because I once had the opportunity to get into his daughter's pants? Is that it?"

We had an audience by that time, naturally, so I said, "That's great, Curtis," to his suit-coated back barging out the door.

I'd been grieving that day over some bad news about the mother of First Baptist's pastor, news I hadn't any business

sharing but which made me heavy inside. But even if I'd wanted to violate pharmacy confidentiality, no way I could've got
Curtis to listen to this worry on my mind. And that hurt me a
lot, that he didn't have an interest in people outside himself.
No wonder I'd asked about Millie; I must've really been asking if he was wishing himself back single again.

We'd had a sort of fight the week before. I'd mentioned to
him here we were turning twenty-five, had got ourselves a nice
house with a yard, and maybe it was time we thought about a
family. I knew that Mr. Sturgis would let me have baby-leave
or at least cut down my hours if I asked. He'd promised that
the day I started work full-time, with my degree finished and
a ring on my finger.

But Curtis didn't have an interest in dependents, four-
legged or two. "Look at my dad," he'd said, waving a bottle
of Bud. "He used to be the one you didn't want to mess with,
the one that the girls lined up for, so I hear. Then what happened? He became *my dad*. What's his name? *My dad*. What's
he got on his mind? Making sure his boy doesn't mess up,
making sure his boy keeps his pants zipped and does not
throw away his chances. That's it, that's his life. I'm not going
down that road, Janey. Not for sure now. Did you think I was?
I don't think we had that conversation. You're the one sells the
stuff that keeps folks from making that mistake. Isn't that
right? Aren't you the one?"

"I just thought, we've been married five years."

"Woman has one baby, man has two dependents."

It was in plain sight. He won the claim for Mr. Dawson: a
ruptured vertebra resulting from a three-car pile up, with serious skidding in a driving rain. He had cause and fault down
cold, though it might take a while, he said, the way claims did,
and he'd need to work close with his client.

By the time Mom called me to say her good friend Madge
at the bank had seen Curtis having dinner with the Dawsons

at the Southern Fried Café, his arm around their daughter Millie who'd driven over from her bank job in Columbia for the occasion, and who still looked as pretty as she had at seventeen, the whole town had passed the news along.

What a feast they'd be having now—finding out Millie had been already pregnant by the time she unfolded that dinner napkin.

6

Dear Mom,

   I thought I'd write you about what I know is of major interest to you and what I hope will get your mind off thinking about the gossip at home. Yesterday, I drove down to Charlotte, which you know is called CharLOTTE up here, to see the little town where Bert Greenwood sets his stories. It looks, as you can see from the pictures enclosed, just like a typical small friendly New England town with the tall church spire and white clapboard city hall that mystery writers love.

   Beulah and I visited the public library and, across the street, the cozy Flying Pig bookstore, and stopped on our way out of town at the old red brick store where the Judge in the books (and maybe Mr. Greenwood in real life!) has his morning coffee. I had a scone, which I am learning to enjoy since it is like a sweet biscuit dough with dried fruit, and took a good look at the other customers.

   Hope you and Daddy are still having nice weather down there.

   Please tell Mr. Sturgis hello for me.

                                              Love,
                                              Janey

I'd gone down to Charlotte for two reasons, neither of which I had a mind to share with my family. One was to give Beulah a chance to learn a new location, walk along new sidewalks (though it turned out there weren't any, the grass coming right to the edge of the streets), and to see if I could spot a poster of Bert Greenwood maybe from a reading at the library or a signing at the bookstore. But the librarian said he never gave readings; and the lady at the Flying Pig bookstore said she always sent the books to Burlington for him to sign.

So I contented myself with snooping around the Senior Center, the focus of *Charlotte's Web,* where old Mrs. Riley falls dead in her T'ai Chi class as if from natural causes. The center looked just the way it was described in the book, boxy and busy, with people playing Mah Jong or taking a break for tea. I even saw the large stone urn on the porch filled to the brim with cigarette butts in which the Judge discovers a cigar stub. The clue which ties the crime to her long-lost brother and heir to her wealth, a scoundrel who sicced a dog on her when they were young, leaving her with lifetime scars. I didn't find the deep backyard with the gazebo where Mrs. Riley's pet pig is discovered loose, letting the Judge know someone has broken in her home. But Beulah had begun to sag with traversing so much grass and with not knowing what her person wanted from her in this new place.

Next time, I thought I could let her try one of the winding dirt farm roads on the back way into town, and take some water for her to lap outside before I had my sweet at the old red brick store, which, this being Vermont, was of course called The Old Red Brick Store.

I HEADED DOWNTOWN in the after-supper dusk the following Saturday, enjoying the heat on the first day that the tem-
perature had been over eighty since I arrived nearly a month
ago. I had on my best white shorts with blue patch pockets on
the back, and my red halter with a sailor collar, showing off a
suntanned back and lots of leg in celebration of summer
weather at last. I had good puppy on her short working leash,
in her nifty orange Companion Dog vest, so she would know
right off that this was the kind of outing where you had to
attend to your name and directions, and different from the
freeplay afternoons on the long umbilical leash at the Dog
Park.

We had been down to the brick streets lined with shops,
closed to cars, before. We'd bought bread from the cute guy at
the fresh-bread kiosk, navigated around other dogs large and
small, and found the fountain across from the Unitarian
Church, (from which Church Street got its name), where
Beulah knew she could not splash, being a puppy-in-training
and therefore not allowed to explore her environment when
she was on her working leash. One late afternoon we'd
stopped at a sidewalk cafe and I'd had a cup of coffee with
milk and a toasted sesame bagel, while she sat attentive by my
chair, not minding that at near-by tables huskies and shep-

herds got to share muffins with their back-packing persons. It was really hard for me, to eat with her just sitting there, but I understood: a trained dog should not be distracted from her duty to her person by the tempting smell of pastrami or fries, nor could her blind person handle a puppy cadging food from strangers.

Beulah liked to have outings, which she was supposed to do a lot, and coming downtown was part of helping her become a mannerly companion. For instance most always there'd be some dog a block away barking, which she was not allowed to do, and although I knew how to put my hand on her throat to stop her while telling her to sit, she'd learned not to be distracted by the other dogs, or by the occasional one who would jump up on its person who then had to shout, "Quit that, no, no, bad dog," words that we never used with our puppies who were raised only with praise.

Most days when we went downtown there wasn't much of a crowd. I'd started noticing a fair number of women with long braids down their backs or over one shoulder, sometimes brown or silver, plus a lot of men with beards, some of them old as time, wearing bandanas around their foreheads. And there would always be a cluster or two of French-speaking visitors come down from Canada. But hardly any blacks, and that felt weird to me, coming from the South: as if I'd landed in a gated state.

This Saturday, however, turned out to be different. Even though I knew it was the Jazz Festival and even though I'd heard loudspeakers calling to us like sirens to come out, I hadn't prepared myself. That is, I hadn't prepared Beulah for about a thousand people at least, wandering around, crowding the outdoor tables, listening to the sounds of clarinets, saxes, keyboards coming from open café doors or over the mikes on high nailed-together bandstands. A *way mixed* crowd brought to town by the music—crowds of blacks (island blacks, African blacks, and downhome blacks), scattered Asians, clusters of tourists speaking in French and German and a language I couldn't guess.

I felt out of place and alien in my red, white and blue American flag outfit, showing four-foot of bare leg and half a yard of bare back, when all the visible females near my age wore ground-dragging skirts or doubled-over army pants riding on the pubic bone and undershirt-style tees in what I guess you'd call vegetarian colors: eggplant, squash, pumpkin, kale, mushroom.

But I tried to enjoy being out and to keep my mind on Beulah, who stuck close beside my leg in the mob, and didn't, the way another dog would, at any time sniff the sides of buildings to see who'd been there before, or try to mark the poles that held up the store awnings, or whine at being down there in proximity to a couple of hundred shins. Trying to make a space between bodies to steer her through, I felt something warm and wet nose around my butt, and wheeled to see a humongous white shaggy dog of immense presence and beauty—looking at my girl as if at a snack. Quickly, I did the defensive move from the Puppy Manual and placed my creamy lab between my calves, protecting her with my body, and said in a friendly way to the rail-thin woman in a long paisley skirt holding onto the outsized hound, "My, isn't he big? Sheep dog?"

"Pyrenees," she corrected, but, spotting my dog, tugged her chummy monster away by his choke collar.

Slowly, I maneuvered us along the strip of shops in the direction of Banana Republic, where I'd seen a red hoodie that I thought would cheer me up and be just right for windy walks along the lake, though I could see it might be too bright to wear downtown. I didn't used to worry about clothes at home—if we were going out, back when *we* meant Curtis and me, I'd change from my white pharmacist's coat into a flow-

ered dress and maybe sandals with heels. And take a little time
with my face, so I'd feel in a party mood and he'd take notice.
Or if he was going to be late, just put on running shorts.

But they'd changed the window displays since I'd last been
here last; now every single window featured Father's Day outfits—khakis and white shirts, white shorts and khaki tees. But
surely fathers didn't buy their clothes at Banana Republic? I
tried to imagine mine, Talbot Daniels, out of his pressed shirt
with no tie for the hardware store, buying an outfit for mow-
ing the back yard or sitting in the sunroom, with his bedroom
slippers on, watching golf, a game he'd never played. But then
it came to me, slowly and with a kind of heavy weight
attached to it, that some fathers were no older than I was, that
some fathers were exactly the age of me. Curtis for instance.
Curtis who would be one before the next time these windows
got dressed up to honor daddies.

In zero seconds, my eyes flooded and having no sleeve to
wipe them on, I used the little cloth bag with cows on it I'd
bought to carry my wallet and keys. Sopping wet quilted
cows. "Oh, Beulah," I sniffed, there in the herds of hundreds
milling by who paid me no mind. And when she looked up at
me, hearing her name, I had to say, "Good girl," and tell her
to sit, and then say it again, because she did.

Then, just as I heaved a sigh and bent to wipe my nose on
the back of the cows again, the person from the Dog Park
appeared, looking just the same: familiar. A comforting sight,
for what did I care what someone like him, with the straggly
face hair and mushed-down hat, thought of my making a display of myself on Church Street in plain sight of legions of the
friends of jazz.

"Janey?" He peered at me.

"James." I held out my damp hand.

"Hey," he bent and spoke to good dog, who seemed to
sense that she'd been in the vicinity of his kneecaps before,

although she glanced around as if looking for his big three-colored dog from the park. He introduced me to another teacher about his age named Pete, the sort of pudgy sidekick with overbite, old remnants of acne, and an eager smile that I also remembered from school. So I liked him, too. And to three of their students with various piercings who claimed their names were Cubby, Wolf and Lobo.

I shook all their hands, wiping mine dry, telling them I was from South Carolina, a foreign country to them.

"I was going to call you," James explained, apparently not bothered that his people were listening in as best they could among the din, "but I didn't get your last name."

"Daniels," I said, "anyway, I'm not in the book; I've just got my cell up here." Then, because I felt warm toward him, for coming along at the right time and acting like he was glad to almost literally run into me, I told him the truth. "I looked you up in the phone book, but there were *nine* James Martins, four of them married." I smiled.

"Hey, hey," one of the kids gave him an elbow.

"It's M-a-a-r-t-e-n." He spelled it for me.

"That's Dutch or something."

"Yeah, they spell it like that over there."

Pete said, "We take students abroad, that's what we do, James and I, the ones doing the summer abroad programs. He does The Netherlands and I do Germany. The Experiment in International Living sets it up for us." He looked proud. "Over there I spell my name *P-i-e-t-e-r*."

I looked at him, and then at James, with appreciation. *World travelers*. It made sense. That's what happened to those boys who appeared in our classes for a few years, got top grades and high scores, and then vanished. They *went somewhere*.

They asked me if I'd like to head up the street with them, but I said, "Puppy's worn out," and by then she must have been.

James hung back after the others started off. "You were, uh, crying it looked like? When we came up?"

I nodded, thumping my cow-bag against my bare thigh. "Yeah, a little, I was. I guess it was seeing all this stuff for Father's Day." I gestured. "In the windows?"

He looked away and tugged his knit cap down over his eyebrows. (A knit cap in midsummer? It must be a local thing.) "Yeah, Father's Day."

"Here," I said, and wrote my cell number on the back of his hand with a felt pen, hoping he wouldn't smudge it too much to read. Then, giving him a wave, I began to inch through the mob with Beulah by my side, letting him think I was some sort of noodley person who would be weepy over her daddy at twenty-five years of age.

For a minute I considered getting a Ben & Jerry's Cherry Garcia cone, but when we pushed our way to their parlor, there must've been fifty-five people waiting in line for cones, half of them outside on the street, two of whom happened to be young, pink-cheeked and pregnant. I didn't need that.

Instead, I turned down a near-empty side street into a warm and gusty wind which I took gratefully in my lungs. And we listened for a minute, catching our breath, to the fading sounds of a wailing clarinet.

When we passed the pharmacy, still open and doing business, I couldn't help it, I had to go in. And if Beulah had been allowed to pee on some car tire in the parking lot and scarf down a people-treat such as a chocolate-chip cookie, I would have stayed till they closed the doors, seeing who came in at this hour with that wrinkled scrap of paper in some doctor's handwriting, who came in just to read the labels on the herbals, needing something for their vague unease. Instead, promising my good dog, whose big paws were slowing and whose middle was sagging, that we'd just do a walk-in, I led her through the automatic doors, knowing she would be welcome in her puppy-in-training vest.

How quickly even the smell, that faint drugstore mix of cosmetics, cleaning supplies, sick people, and drugs, made me stop dead still and have to close my eyes with homesickness. After all, it hadn't been my *job* I'd run away from; it hadn't been the people who needed me every week of their lives to stay of sound mind and ambulatory. Who else could they get down there who'd know what I knew about everybody? No one at all.

Back out on the sidewalk, I stood stock still a minute calming down. That asshole Curtis, of all the wrong-hearted and wooden-headed things he'd done to me, including knocking up his old high school squeeze, this had to be the worst. Making me leave my work had to be the worst.

8

BEULAH AND I trudged up our steep hill, the faint sound of horns and strings following us, the lake reflecting stars behind us, and our driveway safe at hand. All at once, I stopped still as a fox. Pulling the leash up short, I put my hand silently on the puppy's head, sending her an urgent signal to stay. What would a blind person do? What would her dog know to do?

Two guys sat on our porch steps, legs spread apart, blocking our way, half a dozen beer bottles tossed in the yard. To go in the front way, I'd have to say, "Excuse me." I'd have to lead Beulah past them. They looked like serial killers, that is they looked like the two hoods upstairs who rented the top floor of our house. They didn't look like big-city criminals; rather they looked like the kind of punk in college who had half a dozen grievances on his mind. Irritate him, press him, ask him to get out of the way, and you got nothing or you got a threat, or, worse, he made a move. The kind who would open their fly if they thought it would freak you out or shove your arm till you spilled your coffee, dump open your backpack, flip through a textbook then drop it face down in the spilled coffee, laugh, make a few comments on your anatomy, and then, just as panic began to set in, take off.

If I'd been by myself, I'd have turned around and headed back downtown to the safety of the pharmacy. But I had my dog. I needed to use my head. This had to become routine, an alternative set of moves for when our way became blocked, so Beulah would get the idea. It made my chest hurt just imagining the scene of a blind lady, starting up her own steps and getting an arm laid on her, a fat belly shoved up against her, a mean voice in her ear: "You going someplace? Nice dog you got there. You gonna let me have a look at your place? You reaching for the key?" I felt a rush of anger like a windstorm.

Knotting my free hand into a fist against my chest as a shield, I led us down the driveway in the dark. Would my blind woman with her diabetic shoes and heart beating steady on its beta-blocker be allowed to carry a snubnose in her bag? Likely not. And no way would a mannerly companion dog know to go for the throat. I figured as long as we weren't in their line of sight, as long as we circled around the side and didn't happen to notice they were doubtless smoking dope, chances were they wouldn't bother to move their behinds off the steps. Or so I hoped.

In the dark back yard, my ears straining for the sound of footsteps, I held my breath and loosened the leash enough for Beulah to get busy in the perfumed air that let her know she was home. But she hesitated, rubbing against my leg, as if to say that she didn't need to go, if I wanted her to stick by me— though by the length of time she took, I guessed she'd been about to pop. When she returned to the steps, I whispered her name, and we slipped up the back stairs into the house. Inside, I threw the bolts, back and front, and leaving all the lights out, gave her a little kibble and then spread a pallet for myself by her bedtime blanket. Figuring that if she wasn't allowed up on my bed, I could at least snuggle down on the floor by hers. At first she seemed uncertain at this change in our routine, and kept looking to me to see what she should do: *person on the floor!* But when I patted her usual place, and said her name again, she gave a big sigh and plopped down beside me in relief.

"Good brave girl," I told her, talking maybe to both of us, and then, still in my clothes, fell asleep. Holding her front paws in mine.

9

BY THE END of the month, I'd got so lonesome I was going out of my mind. Sitting in my kitchen staring out at the flowering locust, I almost wished I was back at the PACIFIC VIEW motel, at least there I'd had interaction with the lady at the desk and the waiters at the fast-food places across the road. At home in Peachland, I'd had a sort of routine, seeing people all day at the pharmacy, asking about their folks or their kids or whoever they were or had been married to, did they trade in the car, how was the new roof going, was their mother-in-law still visiting. And then bringing home to Curtis a couple of stories that didn't violate anybody's drug-use privacy for him to savor along with the fried chicken or barbequed pork I'd readied for dinner. Then Mom would call, passing on the latest from her best friend Madge at the bank, with whom, when they weren't meeting for lunch, she talked to on the phone about five times a day. Then Daddy might get on the line, to reminisce about when the hardware had been the very heart of commerce in Peachland and in every southern city to the best of his knowledge and surmise.

I called Mr. Sturgis at the pharmacy almost every day. Asking about Mr. Grady's health or how Mr. Haynes and Blind Dog were doing, or what had happened with the Baptist preacher's mother lately, what was he giving our best doctor,

Bayless, for his lungs which were tearing apart? But he gave me short answers, implying that if I was all so interested in my customers how come I'd left and gone halfway to the North Pole?

Finally, desperate for company, I phoned up my mom's Aunt May, thinking that she couldn't have asked me over even if she'd wanted to (though I didn't think she did), since I hadn't had the nerve to give her my cell number. My plan was to call on her if she sounded even the least agreeable, and, this time, to bring a nice gift, maybe a box of Champlain Chocolates, or even some fresh flowers from the stall downtown, though that would require her to hunt out a vase. Something like the deep red peonies blooming in the yard next door, which I could smell in the early morning when Beulah and I sat a while on the steps, and which you couldn't grow in South Carolina. And this time, I wouldn't bring my puppy along.

"Aunt May?" I could feel my voice crack a bit and my face flush, since I figured she wasn't over-eager to hear from me again.

"Do give me another chance, Janey," she apologized, after I'd asked if I could maybe drop by a minute this morning, and how was she getting along. "I've had something of a shock. Perhaps you saw in the paper? Where the police it seems, not here at any rate, but in a large city, have had titanium teeth installed in their German shepherd attack dogs. Bert has been most upset—it's quite got me out of my usual routine. Some other day, then?"

"Sure," I said, "gosh, that's awful." And it made me wonder if Mr. Greenwood did really live with her or if they were just close and he came over when he got upset about something that might end up in one of his stories.

So when, a couple of days later, the phone rang and it was James from the Dog Park I was really glad to hear from him.

"Uh," he said, so I knew right away it was him, "you want to come over and see my place, maybe? We could go eat or something? I mean sometime? This afternoon? You could bring your dog. If you want to."

And that made me feel grateful toward him, his knowing that my good puppy needed to have outings and see people, the same as I did. So I said, "Sure," and got out my map.

Burlington was shaped like a boomerang, opening out onto Lake Champlain, the north end of town curving around Appletree Bay, the south end around Burlington Bay, with five green and public parks scattered along the irregular length of the waterfront. The streets, as I knew from finding Aunt May's house, were heavy on the names of trees—Linden, Oak, Cherry, Walnut, Aspen, Hawthorn, Maple, Tamarack, Chestnut, Butternut, Willow, Birch, Poplar, Elm, Hickory— most of which I still couldn't identify.

It felt good to be driving again, since I didn't do that much up here, unless we were going to the park to play with other dogs, or I was going to the market I'd found that had free-range fresh chickens and Carolina peaches. I went South on Pine, and, after a ways, turned west on Butternut, which took me into a small industrial area that led to a neighborhood cut off from the rest of town by railroad tracks and by fields on either side. Going up a rise, I blinked to see the road appear to run right into the lake, with nothing, not even a fence, between me and the blue Adirondack across the water. And when I stopped the car to stare, no one honked at me, since there was not another car in sight.

Turning onto Hackberry, I crawled along checking the house numbers on old two-story and one-story shingled homes, rundown, with patched roofs, small yards, porches blooming with planters and window boxes, all facing an empty grassy public playground with a slide and tire swing and a lot of space to play ball. It looked for all the world like a company town, like this was where factory workers had once lived a century ago, when this was a lumber port. I was thinking that I must be turned around, that maybe I headed the wrong way off Pine, when I saw James in the yard of a freshly-painted, robin's-egg blue cottage.

"Hi," I said, a little nervous, getting Beulah out on her loose leash and waiting with her at the curb. I'd brushed my hair straight, and worn my new red hoodie with a white tee and cropped white pants, and tried to fix up a bit. But I hadn't been on a *date,* if that's what this was, in what seemed like forever, and never on one with somebody I hadn't known since grade school.

"Hey," James said, giving Beulah a greeting and outstretched palm. "You found it."

"I didn't know this area was here—." Past his house, I could see a narrow yard, sloping to the lake, grown up in wild grass.

"Pete and I found it, or I did. On my bike. I'd started riding at the Dog Park and I followed the bike path to see where it went, over that wooden bridge, you know, past those condos and docks? Then I ended up here. Pete wanted the place in back, it used to be a garage. We fixed it up, did I say that? It took a lot of work."

He wiped his forehead, then smiled, as if he just remembered you were supposed to do that. "We'd been looking for something. We didn't want to be roommates, at twenty-seven."

"You're a kid," I said, surprised that he was older than I was. He didn't have that lived-in look that came, I guess, with marriage.

"I guess everybody's a kid till they have kids." He shifted his shoulders and experimented with a grin.

I liked that idea. Picturing Curtis Prentice, former stud, becoming a daddy. Dropping by the pharmacy with combed-over hair, his mind on the risks of adjustable rate mortgages and the fact that his wife Millie was putting on weight. Turning into his own daddy.

"You wanna see where Pete lives, in the back?" He led us down a narrow gravel driveway and pointed to a former one-car garage, also painted bright blue, with a window set into the front and also the back, so you could look right through to the water. Then we walked back to the cottage, where, taking an audible breath and fiddling a minute with his watch strap, he led us up the steps and through his front door.

Those guys in school who sat in front of me, the ones like James with layers of old t-shirts and Klondike shoes, who aced their tests and went off, or so we heard, to serious schools and later fame—they had no other existence for me but the classroom. Since I had never gone out with one, they seemed to me to exist like the chalkboards at school, coming to life when the janitors turned on the lights. Now, inside the home of one, what had I expected? A heap of flannel shirts (this being Vermont) on top of a cot, a couple of calculators, fourteen pairs of shoes and wads of dirty socks and a bathroom you didn't dare enter.

Instead, the place was beautiful; I felt Beulah should wipe her paws. Gleaming wood floorboards sanded smooth as velvet, the old nails hammered flat and shiny. In the room we entered, James had a polished wooden desk and facing it an elderly rust-colored settee and a black-painted straight chair which matched one at his desk. On the wall, he'd mounted a pen and ink drawing labeled OX HOIST, quite technical and baffling to me, with arrows indicating elm drums, ash wheels, chestnut poles, walnut tubes, elder rollers. And, below that, a smaller ink drawing on heavy paper of a CRANE, with instructions for eight pine beams, two elm trunks, and one large walnut tree for screws. Also on that wall: a closed door. To his bedroom?

I had entered a different country. But then I'd never gone into a man's house before, not one he had done himself, not a place he'd made for himself to inhabit. Curtis and I had gone from our folks' houses to student rentals and then, back in Peachland, to a two-bedroom of our own. A small house we'd tried to fix up more or less in the style we were used to. In that way, I guess we'd been still kids, no longer living at home, but not grownups who knew what they wanted.

While I stood taking in this glimpse of him, James put down a towel and a bowl of water in the kitchen for Beulah, turned on a tape of a deep raspy voice singing "I'm Your Man," telling me we were listening to Leonard Cohen, then changed his mind and turned it off again.

"You want some orange juice?" he asked. "Or a beer or something?"

"Are these for your students?" I asked, gesturing to the elaborate drawings, thinking maybe these were details from famous structures abroad, having to do with cathedrals or mills or some other ancient building they'd be studying. Getting comfortable on the settee and tucking my feet up, I was wondering if maybe all teachers had stuff like this. He didn't seem like any teacher I'd ever had, though maybe I'd have benefited from one like him. Could I imagine Janey Daniels, playing basketball but wishing she was a track star, going into a class taught by a Mr. James Maarten? It would have gone over my head. Though maybe later, in the university, when I'd got serious about learning the specifics of pharmaceuticals easing the discomforts of the body, I might have been curious, attracted, by a course that offered such attention to detail, might even have raised my hand to ask Mr. Maarten, "Why *ash* for wheels? Why *elm* for drums?"

"Sort of, I guess, in a way." He gave us each a glass of orange juice, frosty cold. A ceiling fan blew a little air; still, it was warm. "I read about this building in Italy, a long time ago, built like that—." He leaned back in his desk chair and pointed at the drawings. "A walnut tree cut up for wood screws. That first time I read it, I lay flat on my back and kept reading it aloud because I couldn't believe it. Work like that. I'd just be reading it in my head all the time. You ever do that? The rollers for the hoist were greased with tallow; the ropes were soaked in vinegar. Well, I thought—I take these kids overseas? It's part of the Experiment in International Living, I did it myself after high school—anyway, I thought this impossible building, this dome, was going up, the craftsman was designing it in his head, *in 1428.* So I wanted my kids to know about that, and think about what was happening in The Netherlands at the same time, that's where we go. And compare that with here—he's figuring out chestnut poles for the hoist, and over here in this country at that time, there's nothing like that." He looked at me, and then had to study his knees, his face flushed with having talked so much.

I tried to imagine reading a book aloud to myself to understand it better. Thinking about him, somebody who'd do that, I decided I hadn't known anybody like this before. I had a hundred questions.

"If you take students in the summer," I asked, "how come you're here? I mean, I saw you at the Dog Park the first day of June."

"Yeah," he said. "We did winter term this year."

"But when you went, back in high school, it was summer?"

He wiggled a finger in an ear. "Mostly we do summer. It depends on where the kids are going when they graduate. It's different, different years." He let his eyes roam the room.

How did he get this way, so brainy, so nerdy? "Where was home?" I asked, trying to imagine him growing up.

He gestured around the room. "This is it."

"I mean—." Didn't he get it? "Where did you grow up? Did you go off to school, before you went on the study-abroad program?"

He looked at me, scowling. "You didn't start with all that at the park. I liked it that you were doing this stuff with the puppy, knowing you had to give her away. Not a lot of people would do that. You didn't do a third degree."

"I was just trying to—get to know you."

"Well, here I am. This is me."

"I mean where you came from, you know, your family, the town . . ." How could he not understand that? "I mean, it's what you do in the south, you ask all about a person's family and where they grew up and what they did when they were kids. It's being friendly."

He waved a hand in the air, dismissing my words. "That's how you learn *class cues*. Isn't that what you want? You want to know if I had a rich dad? Do I come from old money, the foreign service, starving artists, film people? That's what you're asking."

"Jeez, James, you must've been through this before. I mean I'm not the first girl you ever had over." Though at that moment I wasn't so sure about that. "Everybody asks questions, don't they? You must've come up with something to tell other people."

"Yeah," he answered, sitting back down, examining a split thumbnail. "I've been through it. Every single female is an interrogation machine."

What was his problem, I wondered. What didn't he want to tell? His dad was in the pen? His mom ran a soup kitchen? Did any of that matter? It did, of course it did, but not like he thought. How could you get close to anybody if you didn't talk about all your baggage? Maybe that's why I'd never gone out with this scraggly face-hair type of guy always putting some kind of cap on his head, always having scabs on his knees, always knowing so damn much stuff. How could you get close to somebody who only sprang to life in Algebra IV or across the ocean?

"Beulah needs to chase her ball," I said, heaving a sigh that must have filled up his carefully bare room. "She needs to get her exercise."

At the sound of her name, precious puppy trotted to my side, and I called her a "good girl," and invited her to "come."

We walked down the green yard to the waterfront edged in reeds and wild purple flowers. Seagulls yelled with their human screech and flew toward town. I'd brought a yellow tennis ball, having first read every scrap of writing on play toys in the Puppy Manual, in case it warned *Never give a Companion Dog a ball to chase.*

"We get winter birds in South Carolina," I said. "Do you feed the ones that stay?"

"Uh," James said. "I guess we will, put out birdseed this winter, me and Pete."

And I held my tongue and didn't ask if this was their first winter here. Instead, I watched Beulah play catch, trotting after the tennis ball as it rolled down the grassy unfenced lawn, bringing it back in her teeth every time I gave her long leash a little tug. She had a fine time; dogs didn't think about the past. *Now* being a yellow ball on a sloping yard; *now* being fetching the ball for your person. James played, too: he lay on his side and rolled all the way to the water's edge with the puppy following along after him, not knowing what to think. *Person on the ground!*

After a bit, he suggested, with the sun slanting low over the mountains across the lake, "We could eat at Irv's. You passed it? When you turned off Pine? Kind of an old diner, with ten kinds of pie. They've got blueberry waffles and sausage from six a.m. to midnight. If you're not some kind of vegetarian?"

"Sure," I said, resolved to help make it work, my first-ever date with a stranger. "Sounds fine."

10

EVEN THOUGH I had read the Puppy Manual from cover to cover and knew the traits the Companions were looking for, as well as the unwelcome habits we were to avoid, I didn't feel the least bit of apprehension the morning of our first Puppy Social. In fact, all I could think about was that Precious Dog would meet lots of other puppies about her age, all learning to be trusty affectionate companions to a blind person the same as she was. It was early July, though still cool as spring at home, and I'd brushed and groomed her creamy coat, and readied us both in a haze of almost dizzy anticipation. Putting on her working leash, as we'd been instructed, and packing her umbilical leash in my bag for playtime, I dressed myself in summertime white pants and a red-striped tee.

For the last month, Beulah had been growing into her big padded paws, her little belly had disappeared, and now she opened her eyes wide and stood stock still at the sound of her name, to let me know I had her full attention. For the last month, too, she'd been bravely putting up with her vaccines (for dysentery, paravirus, and rabies), taking her heartworm medication, and then, as a sort of reward for us both, each evening before bedtime flopping down on our rented rug, on which I spread a clean sheet, and letting me feel all around her eyes and mouth, rub her gums, run my fingers between her toes, and stroke her smooth tummy—a gentle massage that got her used to human touch and got me used to *seeing her*, the way a blind person would, *with my hands*.

We were meeting for the Puppy Social at what had once been the Country Day School, a daycare facility for preschoolers, and, driving south, with Beulah on the floor of the front seat where Companion puppies had to ride, I found that the turnoff was a road almost due west of PACIFIC VIEW. As I passed the gas station and then the motel, I slowed down and waved, as if at an old friend, thinking how frantic I'd been while staying there, to find a place to live, to get my puppy. Pacific View, Vermont. That seemed like years ago instead of scarcely two months.

Getting out of my car, letting Beulah have a busy break before we went inside—over in a brushy area which one of the Companions steered us to—I expected everyone to be feeling the way I was, thinking we'd all sort of show off our dogs and say nice things about other people's dogs. But the ones who had been to Puppy Socials before had a different attitude, one that seemed to treat the event as one more hurdle.

We all went inside, putting the loose leashes on our dogs and taking our seats in the small kindergarten-size chairs set in a circle, in a large bright room with red vinyl floors, blue-checked curtains at the low windows, and a poster of giant yellow sunflowers facing the door. The Companion leader, Betty, a woman perhaps in her fifties, with a wonderfully easy way of greeting the puppies as if she'd raised them all, made the introductions—though I didn't get anyone's name at that point, not even the names of the puppies, all of whom were labs except for one golden retriever, for staring all around at what I hoped would be new friends for Beulah and me.

She had us bring our dogs to attention, walk them around the room twice on their loose leashes, very fast the second time around, and then have them sit beside us. Then, being very friendly and casual, she went over with us why we'd been brought together, explaining it was not only to socialize, although that was the emphasis for today, but so that we could catch at an early stage any of the potential problems which had to be noted and corrected before they became real problems. Flipping through the thick paperback copy of the Puppy Manual, she reminded us to watch for those behaviors which could prevent our puppies from getting to work: *building worry, growing fearful, becoming distracted,* and *soliciting approval.*

I guess I only half-listened, being so sure that Beulah was Perfect Dog. But perhaps all new first-time raisers started out with that idea. And I felt relaxed, at least I tried to, while Betty finished her talk, reassuring us that what she was saying would become clearer in time. Moving around the room informally, she had us take off their leashes—and let them loose! What a thrill! The dogs who had done this before seemed to know they could bound around and jump up on each other and roll on the floor and nip and chase each other, but the young puppies like Beulah and Edgar, the golden retriever, had a harder time figuring out how to romp and be rowdy, and they mostly watched.

Betty passed out green tennis balls, yarn balls, and Nylabones, and the older puppies wrestled for them with their teeth and that seemed all right to do and reminded me of the big dogs at the Dog Park. Then, after a while, we called them to our sides and to attention, and Betty announced it was time to trade dogs.

Trade dogs? I had trouble getting my mind around the idea. How could Beulah understand another person? How could I give commands to another dog? But I went along with it, and received a small, curious black lab named Naomi, who sniffed my shoes and tried to dig her nose into my bag. But I called her name, and told her "down," slipping a hand under her front legs and pushing her gently, as we were supposed to do, till she rested on her stomach on the floor. Except that she wriggled away and went off to sniff the far corner, just at the very moment that Beulah came back to me and leaned her warm head against my knee. She had been assigned to a hunky guy whose big yellow lab kept trying to mount every dog that came near it, male or female, so I couldn't exactly blame her for wandering off. But then generally the switching hadn't gone well: a nervous lab larger and paler than Beulah stood frozen to a spot behind her person's chair and wouldn't move; a small black lab across the room puddled on the floor as her male raiser watched, turning red; and Edgar, the golden retriever, went looking for a tennis ball.

Then Betty, in the very chatty, low-key way that I now found terrifying, perched on the edge of a table and pointed out to us that we had wonderful puppies who were bound to be good companions, but they had a way to go. She told the raiser of the big aggressive lab that his dog would have to overcome his mounting problem, since companions were never neutered until after they were selected, in case they were chosen to be breeders. And explained to the person of Naomi, the curious puppy I'd had, that she needed to be taught to focus and attend, and gave her some pointers on avoiding distraction. To the heavy-set man who belonged to the black lab who puddled, she suggested that maybe he left her alone too much, that she was growing fearful—"notice how she tucks her tail under"—and that four hours a day was too long to stay away. She pointed out to the golden retriever's person the flakes on his coat, the *dander*, or dandruff, a telltale sign, she said, that he was building worry. "He needs to get out more, take him with you to your children's schools or to the super-market."

All this time I'd been holding my breath. Wanting her to say that Beulah was their prize puppy and to watch how well she was doing. But, instead, and my face burned hot when I heard it, Betty walked over to me saying, "She's soliciting approval, don't you see? She looks to you for your responses instead of making her own." And, to demonstrate, she called Beulah's name, at which my puppy turned her gaze in my direction.

After we'd put our dogs back on their leashes, Betty said to the raiser with the pale dog who still stood frozen, "Maybe she and Naomi should switch. Why don't you two work it out, trade them for a night?" And, while my head was still buzzing, she called me over with Edgar's person, a woman named Sylvia, and said, "We'll let Beulah and Edgar wait a few weeks, and then we'll work out a playdate for them. Edgar's basically doing fine, but he needs to get out more. And you're doing well with outings for Beulah, but you don't want her being so solicitous of you. You don't want her getting too attached."

We all went out to our cars, and everybody else drove off, leaving the two of us who remained to talk a minute by our cars. Sylvia, a dark-haired woman maybe in her forties, in a long woven skirt in eggplant and oatmeal colors, sounded discouraged. "I *try* to get out more with Edgar, but I've got kids, and my husband . . . These people think you've got nothing else to do." I guess I sounded pretty down, too, when I protested, "But I thought you were *supposed* to get them attached to you. I thought that was the point." Still, we shook hands, and traded phone numbers, and the dogs wagged goodbye.

Driving home in my Honda with the Carolina plates, I consoled myself with the thought that if Good Dog didn't get to end up a companion to some worthy and needful blind person, but got returned to me, she could ride up on the passenger's seat beside me as we trekked all the way back to Carolina (a warm and steamy world she had never known), and at night she could sleep on the foot of my bed, and in the mornings lick the last of the scrambled eggs off my plate. Cheering myself up. Not wanting to deal with the knowledge that I needed to start learning to wean my puppy just when she'd stolen my heart.

Building Worry

11

AUNT MAY CALLED me on a Monday in August to actually invite me over. "I haven't been the most hospitable of kin," she confessed. "I thought perhaps, Janey, if you were free some afternoon this week, we could have a proper tea."

"Would today be all right?" I didn't want to seem too eager, but, as I explained to her, "This afternoon, Beulah, my dog, is visiting with a friend named Edgar. So I could come, you know, without her—."

"That's thoughtful of you, dear." Her voice picked up. "Do come this very afternoon, certainly. At four? I haven't been entertaining, to tell the truth, since I went part-time at the library. It seems the more time one has . . . ."

"That's good," I said, "and thanks. This is a real treat for me. I guess I've been getting a little homesick, probably it's this heat that reminds me of Peachland. I miss the pharmacy especially. You always miss your work, don't you?"

"Indeed," Aunt May said.

I didn't intend to share with her that I'd been worrying about not doing a proper job socializing my lovable puppy, since I knew she had a blind spot about dogs. But Edgar's person, Sylvia, and I had been helping each other out. When it was your turn to be the puppy-sitter, you took them both, but let them play together and nap inside, since we didn't figure a blind person would be walking two dogs. And, at the start, Sylvia and I would have a cup of coffee and a short people visit, which I looked forward to. She made watercolor greeting cards of Vermont scenes which she placed in local shops. It happened, she told me, that the more people used email and cells, the more art and craft went into the ways to make paper. I'd sent a box of her notecards to my mom—purple, red, green, blue washes of the lake and mountains. I'd even enclosed stamps, because a trek to the Post Office was something my mom thought you made once a year at Christmastime to mail packages, and not worth the trip just to send off news you could say over the phone.

This time, I resolved I was not going to screw things up with Aunt May, arriving, the way I did last time, in scruffy shorts, unannounced and empty-handed. This time, after I took Beulah to her playdate with her new friend Edgar, I stopped by the flower stall on Church Street and got eight fully-opened roses in yellow and reds, August colors. And then, freshened up and in my long white pants and a nice red tee with a little scalloping around the neckline, I left for her house in plenty of time.

Aunt May welcomed me at the front door and took the bouquet. She had on cropped tan trousers with a fresh white shirt with deep pockets, and tan cords on the glasses that hung around her neck. The last time I'd been here, the only time, we'd sat in her rug and book-filled front room, *the receiving room* as my grandmama, her sister, would have said. But this time she'd spread a real cloth in the dining room with one plate of what she said were cream scones and another of tiny pimento cheese sandwiches. A real tea. I felt my eyes fill at finally being invited over in a way that I'd expected the first time. I could even smell the tea leaves, steeped way stronger than I liked, but there was a pitcher of real cream as well as lemon slices to help me out. Seeing what she'd done, the trouble she'd gone to, I did have to admit it was better I hadn't brought Beulah and had to keep her locked a long time in the hot airless car.

"We'll wait a moment or two," Aunt May said, popping my eight bright roses in a mason jar and putting them in the center of the white cloth. "I've invited, I hope that's agreeable with you, Janey, a friend of mine who lives in the carriage house out back, to make it more of a party."

I admit I felt a rush of anticipation. Could it be that I'd actually meet Bert Greenwood? Mom would have a duck! I wanted to ask, if that was proper to do, where his bad view of dogs came from, and if he'd ever once put a good dog in a story. I'd now read two of his books—the one about the retired lady whose brother had sicced a dog on her when she was young, leaving her with lifetime scars, and the one in which a woman whose wrongly convicted husband survives being mauled by a posse of prison dogs. Both times, the judge who solves the cases, Judge Caldwell, retires to his chambers for a jelly glass of bourbon to help him get his mind over the awful event. You had to like the judge. He had big feet which resisted wingtips, and, naturally, happened to be widowed, the way most private eyes were, so they could be thinking about some female and make it clear they were not living alone by inclination. Then the librarian lady he's seeing has to look up old cases for him to peruse so he can fit the pieces together and bring the guilty to justice.

Then we heard the back door open, and I followed Aunt May into the kitchen, though she might not have intended me to. A small woman with tight gray curls, glasses and a flowered violet dress came in and set down a basket of fresh peaches. "This must be Janey," she said. "The niece. You're the niece, aren't you? What a resemblance, you two." And she looked across to where Aunt May and I stood, each a head taller than she was. She gestured to the basket. "I thought you might be missing peaches, being from Carolina, although I'm sorry to confess these are from New Jersey."

"I know," I said, reaching out to shake her hand. "They call them eastern peaches in the market and they're delicious—*Jersey peaches*." I laughed because that sounded such a contradiction.

Aunt May introduced the woman, "Janey, this is Kitty Boisvert who lives in the back. Kitty is a local historian, rather, a historian of the local area."

"Sooner or later," the small woman said pleasantly, her teeth slightly crooked, "historians always end up beholden to librarians."

"I'm glad to meet you," I said, staring at her, trying to be friendly and not let my disappointment show.

"Come on, Kitty," Aunt May said, "peel a few, then, while I ready the tea."

"May," Kitty talked as she slipped the fragrant fruit from their skins, "I got a call on my machine from a Mr. Levine—."

"Levine?" Aunt May considered. "Offhand, I'm sure I don't—."

"The things I can't remember." Kitty wiped her hands. "I leave these messages for people and then when they call back I haven't the foggiest. I guess I could look him up in the phone book, see what he does, anyway, where he lives. But there've got to be at least sixty Levines in the phone book, I'm sure."

"That's nice," I murmured, thinking as I often did up here that I hadn't really got to know my temporary home yet.

Aunt May stopped, teapot in hand. "What's *nice?*"

Kitty threw back her gray curls and laughed. "She thinks they're Jewish." She looked at me, still laughing.

Aunt May laughed, too, shaking her head while I turned red with embarrassment. Because of course that's exactly what I had thought. She explained, "It's L-a-v-i-g-n-e, Luh-veen, a common French Canadian name. It means vine, grows everywhere. There's a—.'"

"—funeral home," Kitty interrupted. "That's it. Lavigne's Funeral Home. I'm doing a little research on mortuaries, those that began in the 19th century or earlier. Times have changed. That's history, how things were. That's it, I remembering calling him, Lavigne."

I turned and studied the kitchen wall, to give myself a little time to cool off, feeling like a complete dunce. But in a town with four synagogues, well, I just thought—*Levine.* Breathing in and out, I read some of the clippings tacked to a corkboard.

Obadian Alwyn
b. Rumsey, England
d. 1878 @ 79

The children of killers are
not killers, but children.
—Elie Wiesel

*The third spear carrier on the left should believe that
the play is all about
the third spear carrier on the left.*
—Lawrence Olivier

Then we all sat in the dining room, at the table with the white cloth, under a cooling ceiling fan. On the wall in front of me, a print of Raoul Dufy's "Open Window, Nice," hung, its window looking out at a lake by a small city such as this one. Listening to the women, I helped myself to a china plate of peach slices, pimento cheese sandwiches, and a warm cream scone. My steaming cup held dark steeped lemon-lightened tea.

Kitty fanned herself with her napkin, saying it must be global warming, that she'd seen an article saying soon it might even quit snowing in Vermont in the winters. Aunt May said that was nonsense, that the last time it had been this hot in August had been 1947.

And all the while I sat there smiling, amazed to be having afternoon tea with my great aunt and her close friend Kitty Boisvert.

12

MOM NEARLY POPPED with pleasure at the news that her aunt had remembered her antecedents and invited a member of her family for a visit. Her daughter Janey, and about time.

I told her all the little details, her and Daddy, who naturally was on the other phone. What I'd worn and that I'd fixed my hair nice, and left my puppy with a friend, and taken a hostess gift of real florist roses, eight for the month of August. "Aunt May set a beautiful table, with a good white cloth, and we had tea with cream scones and little pimento-cheese sandwiches."

"Did I ask you for the menu? The item you promised to relate about the *belated* visit to my *only living kin* was: Did you meet her beau? What did he look like? You can't tell squat from the book jackets. They always show him walking off into the trees, that's the trademark, you might say. Did he and May get cozy?"

Daddy interrupted, "Your Aunt May, cozy? You've must've got her mixed up with somebody else, Ida Jean. She's a librarian. I'm saying that's not just a job, it's a personality is what I'm saying."

"No," I told mom, "Bert Greenwood didn't join us. I believe he—isn't much for socializing. Writers are that way. She mentioned he'd got upset recently about an article in the paper on attack dogs . . ."

"What did I tell you, hon, I read all his books."

I cleared my throat and took a swallow of iced tea, wanting to give a little pause so they'd be listening—that is, if they wanted to hear what I was going to say. Beulah sat beside me on the living room floor, a fan blowing our hair. "A woman historian joined us, a friend of Aunt May who is doing research on funeral parlors."

"A subject we do not want to hear one more remark about: funeral parlors."

Mom lowered her voice. "What's this about you're seeing this James somebody that you just happened to mention you've been seeing?"

"He's from Vermont; he's a teacher. OK?" Of course they were going to ask a thousand questions, which I should have foreseen before ever mentioning him.

Daddy broke in, "How about his folks, where are they? What do they do?"

"I believe they're—in the dairy business," I said. Cows, Vermont.

"Farmers? His family's got a spread with milk cows? You don't think of a cold place having grazing."

Mom hushed him. "Give the girl a break, Talbot. She's got a boyfriend maybe who happens to be someone else from the someone here who she spent the last five years of her life married to. That's the number one and only thing we need to know."

"You look after yourself," Daddy said, "hear me? You understand?"

Mom had the last word. "The next time you go over there to see her, you could take along one of Mr. Greenwood's books, that's nothing but a compliment, which I'm sure he'd be glad to sign to be accommodating to someone that's in the family."

13

Dear Mom,

I thought you and Daddy would like to see some different photos of Charlotte than the ones I sent before, and hope they will get your mind back on a matter of major interest to you and off the teacher named James, who I know only in a friendly way.

Here is the big clock on the outside wall of the old red brick store which has the Woman in the Moon on the face and different objects for the hours. So the Judge can remember that he heard the gunshot at half-past frying pan before the parade began. And here is his house, which I figured out by counting the ones he passes every morning on his way to enjoy a cup of coffee with his neighbors: the one with the gazebo, the one with the greenhouse, the one with the turrets on top. And the white frame building is the old meeting house where he has his office. Now you can see the locations as you read over the books.

Take care of yourselves, and eat lots of summer peaches for me.

Love,
Janey

What I didn't mention to my family was that after having had the nice tea with Aunt May and her friend Kitty Boisvert, I was wild to get back to Charlotte to hunt for some connection between the books and the women.

On the way, though, wanting it to be a learning trip for Beulah as well, I took a back road off the highway so she could have a walk, a trudge really, on a winding dirt lane between an apple orchard and a horse farm. After all, there was no guarantee her blind person would live in a city with curbs, traffic lights, and crowds. She might wind up the companion to someone used to rail fences, livestock and farmland.

Once in town, Beulah perked right up. She had been here before: *lots of grass, no sidewalks*! I headed us straight for the library, having reread the part of *The Prisoner of Charlotte* where the Judge hears a gunshot just as the fire siren goes off, the ambulance wails, the town clock strikes ten, and a parade of a hundred school children with drums marches down the street and around the landmark one-room schoolhouse. When a prominent citizen turns up dead on the steps of the Congregational Church a short time later, the Judge recalls another wrong-doing committed under cover of a similar deafening din: a falsely convicted prisoner set upon by dogs during a raucous prison riot. And—this being the part that interested me now—he walks down to ask the librarian with the curly gray hair to look up the old news account of that miscarriage of justice, and confirms that he has found the secret past of the dead man, and a lead to the killer.

Afterward, the two chat together about the morning's parade: "*A cacophony of sound*," the Judge declares. To which the librarian replies, "I would rather have called it *a dissonance of noise*." And standing in the well-lit library while the lady at the desk admired Beulah's Companion Dog vest, I could imagine hearing plain as day the voices of Aunt May and her friend Kitty, because that's exactly the way they talked. Maybe, I decided, Bert Greenwood wasn't Aunt May's boyfriend at all but a friend to the two women instead; perhaps they both helped him out and he put them, disguised, in his mysteries.

14

JAMES HAD BEEN to my house before, coming by to get me to walk downtown to meet Pete and the kids who hung out with them. A couple of times he'd walked me and Beulah back here, if it happened to be late and already dark. And he'd hang out with me on the porch for a bit. Not the way hanging out on the porch meant at home, because for one thing I didn't have a swing or even chairs, and for another the two tenants above me—the creepy looking guys who couldn't possibly be students—were liable to come clattering down the stairs at all hours, leaving beer bottle empties in the grass, making cracks under their breath.

But I hadn't invited him for supper before. Meaning that I hadn't asked him over before to spend the evening, letting whatever happened, happen. I knew at least he wasn't the kind of person who would make me nervous entertaining in my marginal and rundown rental. Males like him, they didn't mistake you for your surroundings. I could count on that. I'd decided on a southern supper, since that's what I did best. Fried chicken, which meant soaking the pieces in buttermilk for a couple of hours, and soft cornbread, since I'd already have buttermilk handy, and at first I'd thought about a buttermilk chess pie, but that seemed overdoing it, and, anyway, with fresh peaches still in the market, you couldn't beat piling them on vanilla ice cream.

So I was confident about the food, but asking somebody over in the evening, I didn't know the rules for here. If I'd been back home, inviting somebody, say, like Ralph Smalley, the basketball player I'd been going with when Curtis came along, I'd have been completely at ease about it. We'd talk about his folks, and then we'd talk about mine, the mutual people we knew, which was most everybody, what was going on in Peachland as far as rain and fruit trees, what was going on in Greenville as far as the influx of foreigners bringing in high tech. He'd ask if I meant to keep on working at the pharmacy, like it was still some after-school job, and I'd set him straight about that. Then we'd eat. And we would have already sort of decided about going to a movie we wanted to see or taking off our clothes in a natural way.

I'd asked James for seven-thirty, that being the current time of sunset. At the summer solstice in June, we'd had over fifteen hours of daylight up here, but now, in August, we were already down to thirteen, and, scarcely a month from now, at the fall equinox, the days and night would be equal. Back home it drove me crazy when people mixed up the solstices and the equinoxes, when it barely took one minute to figure out that the equinoxes were when the sun crossed the equator and the solstices were when the sun was farthest from the equator in one direction or the other.

People didn't realize that pharmacists had to be observant of the movements of the sun, and I know Curtis thought it was me talking astrology, but we did get triple the business of antidepressants in the summer months at home, when it got hot and muggy and you got sunburn and mosquitoes. Then, with the approach of autumn and football and the first sightings of tourists, everybody felt undepressed and we were back to the usual alimentary ailments.

The truth was, all I really wanted from this evening was to climb in bed and rut around with somebody I'd never been married to, get all tangled up with each other until we were both too worn out to do anything but drag ourselves into the kitchen, followed by a sixteen-hour nap. But how spontaneous could screwing our brains out be in this place? Having to yank the sofa apart and unfold the stiff metal hinges so it could become a lumpy double bed. Saying to James, "Excuse me, give me a hand here, could you, I'm throwing my back out."

At the same moment that the clocks downtown struck the half hour, I heard him knock on my door. That made my heart swell a bit. Had he been driving around the block until it was exactly time? Did he park by the waterfront in order to have a run first along the lake? I'd wanted it to be dusk when he arrived, figuring it would be really dark by the time we finished eating, so that nobody could stand out front and peer through the windows. I didn't like the fact, for entertaining a man, that my living room, which was also my bedroom, sat half a floor up from the ground and faced the street. Not that I thought the students from the university or the college would be looking in as they barreled down on skateboards or jogged up the sidewalk, still I didn't like being on view. He looked spit-clean and held out a bunch of black-eyed Susans which he confessed came from the waterfront next door to his. When he followed me into the kitchen, stopping to pat Beulah and let her remember his shins, he saw a jar of black-eyed Susans already in the locust-view window. I admitted that I'd picked mine from the neighbor's side of the driveway. And we smiled at having had the same impulse and acting on it.

"Something smells great," he said, handing me his bouquet which I put in a jar next to mine.

I could compare him to boys I'd known in school all I wanted, and make fun of his nervous habits and how he had arms that wrapped around his body a couple of times, but the truth was: he looked good to me. And I liked it that not only was he tall enough to look me square in the eyes, but that he'd started to do that, instead of down or away, even when I forgot and got personal.

We took bottles of Magic Hat out on the back steps, since I'd just heard the upstairs guys squeal out of the driveway in the truck and knew we wouldn't be harassed by them tonight. We let Beulah play around in the cool evening grass on her long leash, fetching her yellow tennis ball and bringing it back to me for another throw, until the sun slipped from sight behind the maple tree next door, and it was time for supper.

Eating with someone was a very intimate occasion. At least it was for me, being not only about the taste but also about the sensual matter of touching the food. Licking just-perfect fried chicken off your fingers, chewing southern cornbread soft as spoonbread, dripping butter, letting the citrusy taste of vine-ripened tomatoes linger on your tongue. And in the air of the warm, small kitchen of my temporary home, the odor of Green Mountain coffee and tree-ripened peaches made a scent that seemed like music. James had another beer and I had iced tea, and Beulah lapped her water, while a breeze came in the window, such a relief from the recent heat wave that it seemed a gift to be grateful for.

So, in that setting, it became the most natural impulse in the world to talk about things that mattered, things that were on our minds. I told him, which I hadn't before, why I'd come up here, what it turned out that I'd been taking a sabbatical from. Including the news at the start of summer that my ex, who'd never given a moment's consideration to the idea of fathering, had decided to become one in a weakened frame of mind.

James swallowed and listened attentively, and I appreciated that he'd come with his head bare, no ratty bandana, no hat tugged down to his eyebrows, his dark hair still damp and combed back. "That the reason you were crying on Father's Day?"

It touched me that he remembered, two months later. I

guess he'd kept the image in his mind of me sniffling into that
soggy quilted cow-purse. "It was," I admitted. "I'd just got the
news."

He finished the last bite of his chicken, wiping up the juice
with a bit of cornbread, and I admired that he didn't mind getting his hands greasy. After considering his plate for a time and
studying the jars of yellow flowers with the black hearts, he
asked, "You want to have kids?"

I shook my head, a sort of waffle, not really yes or no. "I
don't know," I said, and I didn't. I looked down at my puppy
and had a lot of conflicting feelings that didn't need to be
looked at, not at this time on what I hoped would become our
first night together.

We took bowls of fresh peaches and Ben & Jerry's World's
Best Vanilla out on the steps, cooled now by a light wind.
James did his usual routine, squirming around, needing to
consider the locust tree under which Beulah was getting busy,
checking to make sure he still knew how to maneuver a spoon
into his mouth, trying to get the spoon to stand up on his napkin. Then he seemed to inhale a lot of night air in order to
make a kind of offering: to talk about himself. "When I, uh,
went over on the International Living program, I kind of did
the same thing. Got away from stuff, the way you did coming
here. Started over. I picked the Low Countries because everyone else had opted for France and Germany, they were the big
ones back then, now it's Asia. Then I got over there and saw
my name—spelled that way, M-a-a-r-t-e-n—all over the place.
There was a café, we had coffee at a café, called that,
Maarten's. And when I came back I sort of dropped the old
stuff. You know?"

"Sure."

"I was gonna learn Dutch. I was gonna go to Dartmouth,
maybe, get some big international degree. But once I started
working with the program, helping other kids get over there,

I never got around to it. I finished school in upstate New York and came here. I been here ever since." He sucked in his breath and then drained his Magic Hat.

I was touched. At what it clearly cost him to open up a bit, admit he had some kind of past. Touched that he shared his own escape from whatever felt bad in his life back then. Looking at him now, white as some patient stretched out on a gurney in Emergency, I felt as if I should check him for signs of life. "Thanks," I said, and looked away a bit to give him time to recover.

Back inside, in the kitchen, I dug my spoon into the last cool bite of ice cream, came over to him and kissed him deep on the mouth. "Sugar helps," I suggested.

In the living room, we listened to Mary Chapin Carpenter singing "Alone But Not Lonely," while Beulah napped at our feet, her face on James's shoe. I talked about how much I missed my work, how I liked watching the days get shorter since we didn't have such shifts in daylight at home, about how my puppy had added a playmate named Edgar to her life. And James went back to safe things, like what he and Pete had to do during the coming school year to get their new crop of students ready to go abroad. I liked him a lot, for going on with his life, whatever it was he'd needed to leave behind. But I'd lost the urge to ask him to help me wrestle the sofa into a bed.

Maybe another night.

15

MR. STURGIS, THE pharmacist back home, phoned me with some sad news. He'd tracked down my number from my daddy at the hardware, so that he could tell me personally. He regretted to have to let me know that Bayless, our best doctor, had passed away. No surprise to Mr. Sturgis, or to me, since both of us had heard him hacking up the lining of his lungs over the phone. Still, sad. Mr. Sturgis reported that he, along with Mr. Grady, Bayless's patient, and a few others, would be serving as pallbears. (That's how he said it: *pallbears*.) I took that last part as good news, since Mr. Grady, who happened to be a black man, might, in my parents' day, have sat in the back of the church, it being Methodist and him used to his own African Methodist Episcopal Church, and people would have said, "Good Morning, Grady," to him. But he wouldn't have been a pallbearer, at the request of the deceased, whose most trying patient he must have been. Mr. Sturgis thought maybe I'd like to contact the widow, Mrs. Bayless. But it wasn't the widow but Bayless's nurse, who wasn't really a nurse, that I always talked to about the doctor's prescriptions, so I did that, I phoned her. She sounded pretty torn up, having lost her job as well as her life's work.

It did me good to get my mind on real events, and tonight, when we were hanging out downtown, I told James I thought

I'd stop by the pharmacy before going home, as a way to pay my respects. We kissed goodnight in front of Banana Republic. We'd begun doing that, kissing hello and goodbye when we were with Pete and the students, not your wide-open mouth, prolonged kiss, but just a hesitation with our lips holding together. Still, Wolf, Cubby and Lobo had to hoot, woo-woo-woo, and nudge and shove and make comments like they'd never seen such a sight, because James was their teacher and belonged to them. He gave me a wave, understanding that sometimes when we met downtown, I needed to head home by myself, that I didn't always expect him to walk me back or drop me out front if he was driving.

Turning off Church Street, I headed along the quiet sidewalk toward the Pharmacy. Beulah, confident because we often came this way, trotted by my side. The air had a fall feel though it was still September, still pleasant, but with a crispness, and across the street in the Methodist Church yard I saw in the dusk yellow leaves already on the maple. I thought I might find something to mention to Mr. Sturgis when I wrote him, something to let him know I appreciated his call, and really was just on a sabbatical and definitely planning to come back, that I was following all the new drugs mentioned in the paper that were in early trials and how they looked as possibilities. Though I guess what I really wanted to do was just hang out inside a pharmacy tonight, just be there, the way some people hung out in discount stores or book chains, places where you could spend hours and you didn't have to buy anything, or really even speak to anyone.

Inside, where Beulah was welcome in her Companion Dog vest, I studied the Herbal Wellness shelves, a much larger section than we had at home, with their familiar products—kava-kava for calmness, L-arginine for male dysfunction, St. John's wort for depression. I picked up something I hadn't seen before, called Senior Moment, and read, in the tiny-print list-

ing, the primary ingredient: *porcine phospholipids.* Hog lard
for brain food? How could a company do that, letting anybody buy it without a warning, someone who might be a vegetarian or Jewish or Muslim, that they were eating pig fat?

Then, with Beulah attentive at my side, I wandered the
aisles. I did the wall-hung cosmetic displays and the shelves of
body lotions and soaps that promised moisture without addi-
tives. I checked men's shaving supplies and the legions of dental products. I looked at the raft of cold remedies, on which
you could spend a whole evening and people did.

Alone, I might have stood in the back by the chairs
reserved for people waiting and watched to see what prescriptions ailing people got filled. Listening to how, just the same
as at home, the old people complained about the cost, the
handicapped in wheelchairs complained about access, and
young girls filling two or more prescriptions blew their noses
a lot. Such drama I was missing. Such lives exposed down to
the lining of the nasal passages and the gut, such discomfort,
such disappointment, such hope.

16

THE PUPPY EVALUATION had me in a state of anxiety. This time it wasn't the local Companions looking over our puppies to see how they were progressing: this time the real evaluators from the Companion Dog Kennels in Massachusetts were coming to assess each of our dog's potential to be trained in earnest to work with the blind. This was a hurdle we raisers would have to go through three times before our dogs went for the final tests at the Kennels at the end of the training year.

Driving by PACIFIC VIEW, I pulled the car in for a minute, just to stop and catch my breath. I'd dressed in khaki pants and a black cotton jacket, so I wouldn't look like I thought this was play. To my surprise, every parking place in the motel held a car, half of them from Quebec, and the NO VACANCY sign flashed on and off. Crowds already pouring into Vermont to see the fall leaves. In late September! When I'd stayed here at the end of May, the place had been virtually empty.

At the former Country Day School, Edgar and his person, Sylvia, greeted us in the parking lot, and we both felt good seeing the two dogs recognize each other, them getting excited the way toddlers did when they saw another small person they knew, and we let them nip and play a bit. Sylvia had been worried about Edgar being the only golden retriever in the class of labs, and, lately, worried that maybe he had a cold. Did dogs get colds? I didn't know. I'd read in the Puppy Manual all the warnings about ear infections, itchy skin, fleas and ticks, urinary infections, lameness, accidental breeding (!), but nothing about colds.

In the cheerful primary room, Sylvia and I sat next to each other for support, and talked in a general way about how things were going. Then the evaluators arrived and introduced themselves. Patsy, in jeans and boots, explained she would be the one walking our dogs through their paces. As her eyes roamed the room, she seemed not to see the persons at all, but to be studying the dogs as possible Companions. Deirdre, also in jeans, a braid down her back, told us she would be the one scoring our checklists. That a perfect score was five, but that no dog ever received a five.

And then our dogs were called out one by one.

"Tory," Patsy spoke the frisky black lab's name firmly and his person led him out. He actually wagged his tail when he stood by her—and it looked good to see a doggy dog. "Bring him to attention and turn him around," Patsy instructed.

The woman tugged at his leash, at the same time saying, "*Tor-y.*" But the dog didn't move. Patsy said crisply, "He needs to know it's time to work. Do you use his Companion Dog vest when you go out? Do you differentiate when he's working from when he can relax? Here, let's give it a try." Then Tory's raiser had to go through the excruciating drill of watching the evaluator walk the puppy around in a circle, keeping him close by her left leg, then stopping him, having him, "Sit," then "Stay," then being handed back the dog for her to do the same thing, without success.

Help me, Jesus, I thought, using Mom's phrase, my stomach knotting up.

While Tory's woman got her checklist from Deirdre, Patsy called out, "Vijay." I and everyone else had seen that the huge yellow lab still had his mounting problem. All the time we'd been having sympathy for Tory, Vijay had been trying to hump first Edgar and then Naomi. Patsy spoke to his raiser, a cocky sort of jock guy, who seemed to think it smart, his big dog trying to be a stud. But to my regret, Vijay did great once Patsy took his leash. He stood attentive, held himself well, looked straight ahead. Twice he led the evaluator up and down the wide stairs in the back of the room, then he stayed, alert, when she dropped the leash and disappeared from his sight into the bathroom. "How is he in traffic?" Deirdre asked. "No problem," the young man said, "except when there's another dog." "We like tough, confident dogs," she told him. "But stop that problem before it becomes a habit." When Edgar's turn came, Sylvia got up quickly, leading him forward, expecting he would do well. We all did—everyone responded to his wide golden trusting face. But right away, we could see something was wrong. Patsy motioned to Deirdre to kneel down at dog level with her. "Listen. Do you hear that?"

"I think he has a cold—," Sylvia said, biting her lip, as if any canine respiratory problem must be her fault.

"I hear it," Deirdre said, and then the two evaluators spoke in low voices while Sylvia, close enough to listen, turned from red to ashen, and looked ready to cry.

Patsy got to her feet and took Sylvia's arm. "He has a tracheal weakness. Most likely in his male breeding line. We should have caught that, although it's sometimes not expressed. He will have to be released from the program." She leaned down to hold Edgar's throat in both her hands, and, even from our small wooden seats, we could hear a wheeze, almost as if he was being choked.

The four of us who were left couldn't go outside with Sylvia and console her, but my heart broke watching her leave. *Good dog. Good boy.* How could you work so hard with a dog and then have it dropped, when it wasn't your fault? Next to me, Rhonda, already a nervous puppy, tucked her tail in and began to pee.

"Beulah," Patsy read the next name on the list. "Let's see how she's doing." She had me walk her around the large room with its bright shiny floor, stop her, have her "sit," go "down" when I swept my hand under her front legs, "stay," which I told her, and then let her walk me across the room. "Good girl," I praised, "Good girl," breathing out in relief. Then Patsy took the leash, and, at every command, Beulah turned to look at me, to see if she was doing the right thing. When she got to the stairs—which she'd been going up and down out back at home since I first got her, *open stairs* at our place—she turned as if waiting for me to come along. Patsy gave me the leash, saying, "Tell her to go." "Let's go," I said, giving a little shake, and up Beulah went, without a pause, and then came as easily down again.

"She's too solicitous," the evaluator said. "She can't look to the blind person for approval; remember that. Wean her." She waved me to her partner.

Deirdre confirmed, "You take her on an outing at least three times a week?" "Yes." "She rides in a car, on the floor?" "Yes." I wanted to get credit for letting her go off to play with Edgar for whole afternoons and for having him over to our place, too. "Is she fearful?" I shook my head. "Let's see," the woman said, suddenly banging an umbrella against the metal radiator, at which Beulah jumped backward. Then she popped the same umbrella open in Beulah's face, at which my sweet dog ran between my legs.

"Bang on a few dumpsters on your walks," Deirdre instructed. "Let her hear traffic. Let her get close to a few scary people."

Patsy grinned and stuck her hands in her jeans pockets. "We're doing evaluation in downtown Burlington next time; scary shouldn't be too difficult."

Let her get close to scary people? I had them living right

upstairs. But I held my tongue and could feel my face burning from their comments.

"Rhonda," Patsy called, as I sat down with my dog and my marked-up checklist. The rest of the afternoon became a blur. Rhonda's person got a discussion of some of the underlying issues involved in the dog's failure to hold her bladder until the designated spot. Sherry, the pale skittish young lab, who was next, froze halfway up the wide wooden stairs, refusing to budge up or down, having, finally, to be picked up and carried. Patsy warned that the puppy could become too anxious to function. "She's building worry, which results in her being less responsive." Finally, the last raiser, who belonged to Naomi, the frisky inquisitive black lab, got a lecture on how to guard against the dangers of distraction.

Yet all three of these dogs went *willingly* along with Patsy, and then, when the two evaluators changed places, with Deirdre as well, going upstairs, out of the building, and back in, and never once checked on their people to see how they were doing.

All the while I sat there with my cheeks hot, looking at the bold handwriting on my sheet of paper:

anxious—note tight ears
solicits approval—looks to raiser for confirmation
lacks confidence—startles easily, look for shedding

———

Outside, in the parking lot, we compared notes. My overall score of 2.8 was just as good (or bad) as everyone else's. But we forgot our problems at the sight of Edgar and his caretaker, who was wiping her eyes on her colorful sleeve, still standing by her car, and we all went together to tell Sylvia how sorry we were.

17

THE NEXT DAY, I called and invited Sylvia for lunch downtown, thinking she might need cheering up.

"Why don't you come here for coffee instead?" she suggested, sounding glad to hear from me. "We could let the dogs play, if you brought your puppy. I need to stick around here after I take the kids to school."

"Sure," I said, and promised to bring us some pastries.

I felt happy not to have to leave Beulah alone in the apartment while I was gone, which I'd been practicing doing. I could never bring myself to put her in the crate—anyway, I figured at her age, six months, that was just for if you had somebody over where she'd be in the way, such as a plumber, and instead I'd leave her on her long umbilical cord, with a rolled-up pair of socks and the yellow tennis ball to play with, and try not to smother her with hugs, so this would get to seem routine: *person leaves; person comes back.*

I took us on a walk to Church Street early, so I could pick up something personal for Sylvia, although I hoped it wouldn't seem like a consolation present. And I found something nice, some apricot-scented shampoo, right away at the Body Shop, which I knew opened before ten, the only place that did, and that kept a sign in the window which said DOG-HOS-PITABLE ESTABLISHMENT, so Beulah didn't have to wear her orange vest. Then, heading back to my car, I went into a pastry shop called Plum's. I'd passed by it a lot, but never gone in, probably because it happened to be right next door to a sort of transvestite thrift shop that featured leather and metal along with fancy second-hand ballgowns, and which tended to be distracting. Plum's had cranberry and cherry scones, but, a surprise, they also had big square *hot buttermilk biscuits*, and I got three—so I could take one home in case we didn't eat them all.

Sylvia lived on a street not too far from the lake, in an area on the way to Charlotte, on a winding unpaved road with a lot of trees that were starting to turn, and with those street signs that had Pvt. before their names—hers was Pvt. Ethan Albertson. At first I'd thought these were named for privates in some war, but she explained they were just private roads. Beulah sat, patient, on her towel on the passenger seat floor, and that made me wistful, that she couldn't ride up front looking out the window, or even with her head sticking out into the wind, the way you saw ordinary dogs do.

I pulled off the dirt road into the driveway of the weathered two-story house, where Sylvia and Edgar were waiting for us. The dogs seemed so happy to see one another that I wished I could just take Edgar myself, now that he couldn't stay in the companion program. I really loved the idea of Good Dog having a playmate all the time. But I had called and asked Betty about that, and she had said that wouldn't do. That he'd been placed already in the Released Dog Program and there would be a nice home for him on a farm in early summer.

Sylvia seemed to like watching the dogs, too, and we took them off leash to run around her living room. She had dressed up, it looked like, wearing a long green skirt and a loose purple blouse with embroidered sleeves, deep colors which reminded me of her art cards, and the room had the same colors and a big pot of dried purple flowers on the mantle. She put out a tray for the buttermilk biscuits—still warm—with a cup of decaf latte for herself and regular Colombian coffee for me, indicating she knew my preference, and that seemed so thoughtful I was touched.

I handed her the Body Shop gift all wrapped in three different bright tissue papers and tied with three matching ribbons, and set my bag on the sofa.

"Shampoo," she said, letting the paper drop to the floor. "You didn't have to do that, Janey. Do you think I need something to fix my hair? I know I do. This time of year it gets dry as hay."

"No, not at all—." I felt awkward, her taking the gift that way. "It was something I liked." Did that sound like I wanted some myself?

"Biscuits," she said, not making a move to try one.

"You must be happy a little bit, aren't you? To have Edgar be really your dog? It wasn't your fault and it wasn't his—and he's such a sweetheart. Anybody would want him." I thought about a dog that could sleep between your knees at night, and lick out the milk from your cereal bowl in the morning. And ride in the car looking out the window, since that was still fresh on my mind.

Sylvia wadded up her bright blue napkin and put in on the coffee table. "I knew I'd mess up. I always mess up. He says there is not one single thing I do that doesn't go wrong. I asked him, 'What about the kids?' He said, like he was kidding, but he wasn't, 'They had me to help.' I wanted to show him I could do something right. Raise a puppy for a blind person, I couldn't get the idea out of my mind. It wouldn't be like having a child, going on and on and on, it had a beginning and an end. Look after it for a year, a little puppy, and then when it got socialized and knew the rules, you let them give it to a blind person. Just to have a job one time that I could start and finish and get right. You know what I mean, Janey? Maybe you don't; you don't have kids."

"No," I said, finishing the other half of my biscuit, wishing but not asking for butter to go with it. "I don't."

She crossed her legs and then knotted her fingers together. "He griped from the start. 'We don't need a dog, we can't keep it all together now.' I told him, 'We're not getting a dog; we're being a prep school for a dog.' I thought that was a pretty smart answer: *a prep school for a dog*." She laughed in a glum way and ran her hand through her dark hair. "Now he's mad at me for the time it took. 'If we'd wanted a gee-dee dog,' he told me, 'we could've got it from the pound.'"

"My mom likes your notecards," I said finally. "She hates to write letters in the worst way, because it means finding a stamp and going out the door. But she says she's actually writing me a real letter to answer mine, on the one with the sailboat at sunset."

"You don't have to say that." She took a sip of her latte, which must've been lukewarm by now.

"You're a good artist."

"Another place on Church Street is interested in carrying them." That seemed to please her.

"Doesn't that count?" I asked. "With him?"

"Nothing you do outside the house counts compared to what you do inside the house. Weren't you married?"

"I guess what I did outside the house actually made things worse," I admitted. It made me sad, things going wrong for her here at home. And sad for Edgar, too, who'd barreled back into the room with Beulah behind him, a faded green tennis ball in his mouth.

"Don't you have somebody you're seeing?"

I nodded, reaching out to pat the two good dogs, and throw the ball.

"Just don't get married again. You give them that, they

own the store."

I gathered up my things. "Thanks for letting me bring her," I said. "I hate having to leave her at home all by herself—."

"You're cute with that dog," she said. "You can tell you don't have kids."

We walked together out to the driveway as a sudden wind whipped across the lake, turning the sky a deep flat gray. Surely not *snow*? While we were still on Daylight Saving?

"Thanks for the shampoo," she said again. "You didn't have to do that."

18

WHEN WE GOT home, figuring Beulah would want to head out to her shady privy under the black locust, I let her down the back stairs. Just as we got into the yard, with her loose on the leash, we nearly ran into one of the scary guys from upstairs in the act of pissing on a small lilac bush in Beulah's corner of the yard. She started to come back to me, startled, and then headed right in his direction, needing, I guess, to get to her spot.

The scroungy tenant, the burly one who looked like a serious drinker, with stringy hair and dark bags under his eyes, turned around and shook his dick off, air-drying it before tucking it in. "Didn't expect company," he said, not seeming to be bothered.

"My dog pees in that corner." I felt territorial.

He turned around to look. "Sorry, I didn't see the sign." He bent down and addressed Beulah, "Don't mind me, it's just family."

I shook her leash a little to let her know it was OK, though how she could have gone right over there and done her business with this menacing guy standing there, I had no idea. I couldn't have blown my nose with him around. I could feel the back of my neck prickle. "Doesn't your place come with a bathroom?" I felt like scolding him, for embarrassing me, mostly.

"Hell, Roland's in the can. I tell him he's impacted and oughta see a doctor."

"You just have one bathroom upstairs?"

"Yeah, you could say. They divided the room, toilet over here, shower over there, like it's two rooms. They rented it up there calling it two apartments, but what can you find this close? The answer's zip." He adjusted his belt. "He know you got a dog?"

"Who? The guy that rented it to me?"

"Lavoie."

"I guess if he wants to know, he can."

"He don't know."

"He *could* know." Did this jerk mean to report on Beulah and take my apartment?

He peered at me. "You're not blind; Roland says he bet you could tell when we're around by the smell, he said he thought you couldn't see. I said, By your smell maybe, not mine."

I laughed. "When she's grown, she'll go to a blind person."

"I told him you weren't."

Beulah had come back but I kept the leash loose so she could check out the scary guy and see that we didn't have to run away. Not yet. "What do you guys do?"

"You mean besides nothing much? We're back in school, the both of us. Roland took a little sabbatical from his studies to fuck himself up real bad, and I got my hide fried getting a nasty divorce as a change from a nasty marriage. You don't look like you know much about that, but I got myself together with a get-down ugly bitch. Once I've got my piece of paper, I can go back to having my own place. My dad was a roofer. It fit him just right. He liked the hard work, and he liked doing it on his own time. He stayed fit; he didn't look a day older when he died. He gave me good advice. When I got into this mess with who's now the former wife, he said, You're thinking with your dick. I said, You got something better to think with? I'd been working for the gas company. I liked driving a truck and being out of the office. I thought about UPS but that looked like too much work. Dad said, Go back to school. Today's world, you got to get a degree. He was right; you want to get off hourly, you got to get the piece of paper."

"I know about that," I told him. "In high school, I worked at the pharmacy back home doing the same thing I do now mostly, but now they've got a name for what I do, and they're holding my place till I get back."

"That's a field for women these days, I see that." He took another look at me, hefted his pants. "How about the dude comes around here? He oughta get you a better place. He can afford it."

"He's a high school teacher."

"Yeah, right. Rich kids can do that, they can grow these little beard jobs and dress like street people. Roland and me see them coming up here all the time from Connecticut, looking like vagrants, except they've got these clean fingernails and custom haircuts. You look, you'll see what I mean. Passing joints in their Doc Martens and showing off ten years of orthodontics."

I shook my head. That wasn't James; he didn't know James. I said, "I guess in the South, it's the other way around—runaways dress up to look like Country Club even if they're stealing to eat."

"We figured you was from down there. Roland said Alabama, he knew a girl came from Alabama."

"South Carolina."

"I grew up in New Hampshire. I'm not proud of that, but I did. My dad moved here and he had the right idea. Roland, he says he's from New York. But I tell him that's New York, Ontario, maybe."

"We better go," I said, gently giving good dog's leash a tug. I'd been standing talking longer than I should have.

"Tell your pup I used the Boys' Room and not to worry."
He held out his hand, big as a slab of ham, rough as sandpa-
per. "Larry."

"Janey."

"Janey. I got that. Remember, you get into trouble, you
pound on your ceiling with a broom handle and we'll be right
down. Though I doubt you'll be getting anything you can't
manage, from the *teacher*."

After he went up the outside stairs, and Beulah and I went
in, I sat a while at the kitchen table, hugging my shoulders,
Good Dog by my chair. My folks had left a message on my
cell, but I needed to think about the backyard encounter. What
I couldn't get out of my head was that here I'd talked to this
scruffy guy, someone tacky enough to piss right out there in
the yard in broad daylight—and I'd learned more about him
and his life in ten minutes than I had about James in nearly
four months.

19

MOM SAID WHEN they called back, "You think your daddy and I are down here listening to Ricky Skaggs and watching football while you're up there not answering our calls, no way to find you, should there be an emergency. At our age."

"Mom." I turned off Reba McEntire singing "Right or Wrong," and tucked my feet under me on the sofa. "You're fifty years old. You're the age of movie stars."

"You're soft-soaping me."

Daddy got into the conversation. "You having brought it to our attention that you are seeing this young man we don't have proper information on, calls for us to have a look for ourselves. I'm no prude, your mother can tell you that, I am not, but this is not yesterday, this is today, and a girl has to think about is she rushing into something."

"Daddy."

"Talbot," Mom interceded. "We have spent the last six months devoutly praying that our daughter puts past events behind her, most especially the recent past, that being exactly what she is doing."

Not able to grasp what they were trying to tell me, I digressed into the breathtaking spectacle of the fall leaves in Vermont. "You can't believe the colors. Or the thousands of busloads of tourists from all over the country who come."

20

JAMES AND I had worked it out so that I could have a run along the bike path at the Dog Park while he walked his bike and Beulah, and then he could ride ahead and wait for us at the wooden bridge that led into his neighborhood while I walked her, taking her off the path at the water's edge, letting her watch the ducks, standing still if they swam close to shore.

Today, he thought we should introduce her to a romp in the leaves, and suggested he park his bike and we'd hike back into the thick stand of hardwoods between the path and the rocky lakeshore. I had her on a long leash, and let her wade through the piles of orange and rust and yellow which came almost to her tummy, though now she'd blossomed into a coltish dog, no longer really a puppy. I had on a heavy sweater and jeans, and so did James, essential under the cornflower-blue October sky. We sort of leaned our shoulders together, watching her. She loved the crunch of the leaves and the surprise of wading through something which rustled and rose around her. Once she snapped at a bright red maple leaf; once she rooted her face down in a leaf-drift till only her shoulders showed. I took half a roll of film. I'd tried to resist the camera—not wanting to get too sentimental about her. But I had a couple of photos of her as a brand new puppy, markers of our first week, and now these would be ones I could stick in letters to my folks and Mr. Sturgis.

Or sit and look at in my old age.

"Did you used to do this when you were a kid, bury yourself in leaves?" I asked James, thinking how grand it must be to grow up watching the hardwoods transform themselves from season to season. In films you saw parents burning pyramids of leaves in backyards filled with children.

"Don't start that stuff," he said, locking his hands behind his head and lowering his chin to his chest.

What stuff? Couldn't I even ask anything as ordinary and sociable as that? Even people on the Witness Protection Program must have worked out answers to did they play in fall leaves. Even the guys upstairs would have come up with something that had to do with their young delinquent days. "Jeez," I said, not wanting to get into a fight on this particular perfect afternoon. "I just had nostalgia for growing up here, which I didn't do, is all. Can't you ever just give me some kid story? You had braces or you fell out of a tree or you got a ten-speed or your feet grew two sizes in one year?" These arguments were the nearest I came to missing the males back home, any ordinary one of which could've come up with ten thousand memories of his boyhood in a flat minute.

"I told you about the study-abroad program." He located a frown.

"You did," I agreed. Slipping Beulah's leash around his wrist, I threw myself again and again into the mound of leaves under the hardwoods above the lake at the Dog Park.

When the shadows made it too cold, we walked her and the bike back along the path to James's place, where I'd left my car in front of his house, which I could still do, though in another month or so there'd be only off-street parking so the snowplow could come through.

"Do you want to drive with me to drop her off?" I asked him. Trying to make it sound casual, that I had arranged to leave my companion for a sleepover with Sylvia and spend the night at his place, in his bedroom which I'd never seen.

"Uh, sure, I'll ride upfront with her." He looked nervous, as if he'd agreed to something that scared him to death and it was too late to back out.

"James," I reminded him, "we decided to do this."

"Right," he said. Stopping on the sidewalk dead still, he pulled his knit cap down over his eyes, till it covered his nose. Then he took off the cap and put it on his fist, making a puppet face, having it ask, "Can I handle this?"

I laughed, but felt terrified enough myself without his help. Having sex with somebody new, for the first time, single? Mind numbing. All I knew I'd learned from or with Curtis. And I didn't want to think about that, about what he had liked, my ex, what turned him on, what he liked me to do and say. The point being I didn't want him there, Curtis Prentice, in this nice man's bed. I just wanted me there.

But I'd decided that we had to take a stab at the sex stuff or else, if we waited too long, we'd turn into buddies. James's pals: Pete and Janey. And I wanted us to do better than that. I wanted him to take off his clothes and to open his bedroom door to me. He didn't need to give me his whole life story, but if he couldn't expose his actual *self* to my gaze and my touch, then I'd better find that out before I got too tied up with him.

So in the late afternoon's slanted New England light, we drove Beulah south of town to her doggy overnight, going slowly along the two-lane state road that led us high above the lake so that we could see the changing colors of the distant mountains, and, close at hand, the blazing red and yellow maples and scarlet oaks. Maybe October was the most beautiful month of the year everywhere, I thought. We didn't have leaves turning like this in Peachland, too great a distance from the Blue Ridge, but, even so, back home in Carolina at this time the sun always seemed the color of butterscotch and you could smell bonfires and think about pullover sweaters and football and getting outside for a walk.

"I could fix us something to eat," James said in the car, after we'd left Beulah playing with Edgar, and I'd given Sylvia a special thank-you squeeze, hoping another dog wouldn't make too much trouble for her at home. "Stew? I can do stew. We could eat out back in the yard and watch the sun go down." He was looking out the window where he could already see the flame-red globe sinking from sight. He was casting about. I could see him wipe his sweaty palms on his jeans.

"Let's eat at Irv's," I said. "My treat." Feeling as nervous as he looked.

"Waffles and sausage?"

"James. Does it matter?"

"I'm sort of having a panic attack, about tonight?" His voice rose.

"I noticed." I reached my hand over and found his knee, keeping my other hand on the wheel. "I don't care what we eat for supper, do you?"

"I might not can—you know, at my place."

"Hey," I said, "I could have asked you over to wrestle my sofa into a bed. Then we could have thrown our backs out and made a lot of noise and had a fight."

"Yeah, but you made fried chicken and cornbread at your place. I thought I ought to come up with something." He turned in my direction, but I had to give my attention to wheeling into Irv's diner without being rear-ended by the car behind us.

But I guess he was right about fortifying ourselves, because after a good plate of country food, we calmed down and held hands driving under the over pass, up the road that wanted to plunge into the lake, until I pulled to a stop in front of his house. I gave him a kiss, turned off the engine, and we went inside.

To, naturally, find Pete waiting for us in the living room.

Holding three longneck beer bottles in one hand, waving the other, his face beaming, he called out, "Hey, hey, people." And gave us the good news: the International Living Center had got an anonymous donation for nearly two million, to help high school students spend their summers in a total living experience abroad. Then they had to talk about that, the teachers—James taking off his cap, Pete running a pudgy hand through his buzz-cut hair, as if the better to air their brains. After they'd considered all the options involved in guessing how much of the funds *their* school might hope for, Pete showed us a new flyer he'd made up, listing which languages the Vermont Foreign Language Bank had translators for:

Arabic, Bengali, Mandarin Chinese, Danish, Dutch, Finnish, French, German, Greek, Gujurati, Hebrew, Hindi, Hungarian, Llongo, Indonesian, Italian, Japanese, Konkani . . .

Then when they'd finished their celebrating and their beers, Pete took a look in my direction, wiggled his hand in a wave, and started edging out the back door, suddenly remembering he had some stuff that needed doing.

"Uh," James said when we were alone, as if he'd lost his train of thought.

I stood face to face with him. "You know I have never even seen your bedroom."

"Well, hey, the only reason I saw yours is you don't have one."

"Thanks."

He decided we needed glasses of water. Draining his, he wrapped an arm around his head, investigated an itch in his ear, took off his glasses to check for smears. "I'm slightly a wreck," he said.

"I noticed."

"We could go to your place?"

"We're here." I'd put on brand new red panties. I'd worn my only good bra. I'd washed and creamed myself like I was doing a nudie movie. The longer we stood around like this, the worse it was going to get. Did he fret about having or not having a rubber? Should I remind him I was a pharmacist and not to worry? "Are we going in there?"

He stood still for maybe ten beats, and then, suddenly grinning and striding across the polished floorboards, he flung open the closed door. "Take a tour. Be amazed. Be disappointed."

It didn't look the way I'd imagined, that was true. On the floor he had a thin mattress with gray sheets and a white down comforter. On the white wall facing us he had a careful scale-drawing labeled DOME, and one small framed photo of a woman. No stacks of shoes, no old baseballs, basketballs or footballs. No girlie or band posters. No CDs or tapes or old vinyls in sight. A shelf along the front wall on the street side held a humongous computer complex which would have made Michael Dell proud. That was his private room.

I put my arms around his chest, feeling his heart scudding rapidly behind the ribcage. He held me like that a minute, and then went over and closed the door, and, suddenly happy, looking as if some switch in his head had said, It's okay, he began to pull the sweater over my shoulders, at the same time gnawing around on my neck.

Relaxing some, letting out a whole lot of air from more or less holding my breath, I bit his lip, found his tongue, and then cooperated in getting us out of our clothes. The room had some faint light from the street, and, somehow, we got the right things in the right places and remembered how it all went, two people doing that fine familiar thing together. And if we didn't move the Green Mountains on their bedrock, at least we made the moon rise over PACIFIC VIEW.

Pleased with ourselves, we lay on our backs, nuzzling feet and touching shoulders. Relieved, not wanting to move, I turned to him and smiled, tracing my finger along his lips.

Taking my hand, he gestured to the photograph on the wall. "That's the woman who raised me," he said. "She died and took my history with her."

21

I COULDN'T GET enough of the snow. I'd been waking early, sitting up in bed, with it now daylight at six-thirty, though that meant it had started to grow dark by four-thirty, sunsets streaking what seemed a mid-afternoon sky, every day losing a minute or two more of daylight as we rushed toward December's winter solstice. Not sure how I felt about the fact that by the time the days grew as long as the nights were now, I'd be back home in Carolina.

This morning, I took a cup of coffee and sat on the outside steps in the first slanted morning light, wrapped in a robe over my sweater, with Beulah beside me, big dog who liked to sit outdoors with her person. The locust leaves had fallen, scattered, been covered in white, and the dark branches now held a pair of crows from the maple next door. (A bad fortnight for them; the paper mentioned it was crow season for hunters. To some people everything was game.) The bare limbs of the lilac swarmed with sparrows all moving at once until it seemed alive, a bird-bush. And since I'd put out a pie tin filled with wild bird food—*nourriture pour oiseaux sauvages* it said on the Blue Seal feed sack—the songbirds had also come.

Above us, on the second floor, the hoody tenants, Larry and the other one, Roland, were sleeping off the night before, or so I imagined them, flat on their backs, mouths wide open, huge snorting noises, foul-smelling breath coming out in jerky gusts. When they came clambering down, all they'd see back here would be the snow and our vehicles, off the street, all in a row in the wide rental drive. The birds, the dog and I would have moved on as the sun rose in the sky.

The thing was, I had to talk to Aunt May about the matter of my folks coming to town. I'd put it off for weeks, the same way I'd kept not dealing with the fact myself that they were really going to be here. I didn't have the nerve to call her ahead, terrified that she'd say this didn't happen to be a good day, perhaps we could make it later, perhaps *after the holidays*. On the other hand, to show up at her door the way I'd done that first time when I hadn't minded my manners, and throw myself on her begging for help, didn't seem like a great idea either.

So it turned out to be nearly eleven by the time the snow crunched under my hiking boots in Aunt May's yard, a sack with two warm big biscuits in my hand. I left Beulah curled up on a blanket on the floor of the car, a big dog who knew to wait and not get up on the seat or bark out the window, or get scared when left alone. I'd already taken her for a walk downtown, to show her how to deal with ice-slick sidewalks. But then that wasn't really progress, because it was still *me* taking *her* on the walk, still me letting her know when her feet slipped a bit and she regained her balance, that she was a "good girl," that she was doing fine. Instead, I knew that I should be teaching her to worry about *my* feet—that is, her blind person's feet—and to be the one to navigate the treacherous sidewalks and noisy traffic on her own.

"Good morning, Janey, this is unexpected," Aunt May said from the front steps, the door open behind her. "Look there," she said, in a friendly tone, "you've made the first tracks on the snow." She considered, frowning. "The boy who brings us the paper must have come hours ago then, before the last flur-

ry. Certainly he must." She looked past me at my trail from
the car.

I handed her the still warm buttermilk biscuits from
Plum's. "I didn't make these," I admitted, "but they taste like
home to me."

"Come in. I'll fix us tea. I should have built a fire on a day
like this. I bring the logs in and then—but who builds a fire in
the morning now that our homes have central heat. Here,
now, shouldn't you take off your shoes? And let me hang up
your wrap."

"I meant to call first," I confessed, wanting her to know I
knew better than to show up at the door, interrupting her
morning. "But I got cold feet."

She looked down at my heavy socks and smiled. "About
what, Janey?"

"I need some help."

"Let's put these on a plate," she offered, taking my biscuits
and heading for the kitchen, with me trailing behind.

From upstairs, I heard a door close and the light sound of
feet retreating across a room. I flushed, realizing that I had
barged in without giving Kitty a moment's thought. Then I
saw, on the dining table, a newspaper article from the *New
York Times* spread out, and copies of articles from the web, all
reporting on a woman who had been chewed to death on the
stairway of her apartment building by a pair of dogs.

"How horrible," I said to Aunt May, following her into the
kitchen. I could not bear to imagine bad dogs in a world which
contained Beulah. How could I ever protect her? How would
she be able to protect her blind person?

"Yes, it is devastating."

"Will this—do you think?—go into one of the mysteries?"
And instantly felt ashamed, to be asking such a thing.

She considered for a moment. "I have no doubt it will alter
the story in some way. Exactly how—." She set out two cups

on a tray, and I saw, relieved, that it would be just us.

I read an item from the local paper, pinned to the cork-board, quoting an expert on wife-abuse:

> Hairstylists are on the front lines, they're the ones who
> see the bruises in the course of their daily work and
> they're the ones who can point people in the proper direc-
> tion to get help.

"Here, now," Aunt May said. "Let's take our hot biscuits and jam into the front room." She looked toward the bay window. "Did you leave your dog in the car, Janey?"

"I did. But she's fine. She has a blanket."

"You can keep an eye on her from here."

"Thanks," I said, surprised at her interest.

We ate the crumbling buttered biscuits and sipped too-strong tea, while Aunt May stared out the window at the snowy yard where even my boot prints no longer showed. I hadn't really looked at her before, as someone apart from being Mom's aunt, but now I saw the lines around her eyes behind her glasses, the gray bangs grown a bit too long, the face of someone with a lot of stuff going on inside. Would I look like that someday? Tall, composed, and a little bit off somewhere else? She wore a heavy cotton gray dress and sweater, and gray socks with what she called sneakers.

"What's on your mind, that brought you out this morning?"

I didn't know how to ask her, or even how to tell her. So I blurted out the whole of it. "Mom and Daddy are coming to Burlington before Christmas, to see how I'm doing up here." I let out my breath. Did she understand what I was really say-ing?

"I see," she said. Looking off, she sipped her tea and then seemed to study the rug at her feet. "You mother will wish to be invited here."

"She will," I said. "She asks all the time if I've, when I've seen you, and if I've met—*him*." I couldn't look at her.

"And if we disappoint her, she'll have a duck." She gave a sigh.

I laughed, since that was exactly Mom's term for getting in an uproar. "That's it."

"When do they plan to come?"

"Ten days before Christmas. They didn't want to miss the actual holidays at home. The church does a lot."

She nodded. "It will be dark then shortly after four. Let me think. We need someone to dilute family here. Have you perhaps a friend?"

"James. I'm seeing a teacher named James."

"Just the thing. An ally for Talbot among all the females. That will make six of us. That's civilized. One is obligated to make general conversation with six. We'll do something in front of the fire. I never have a tree; haven't for years. But holly and wreaths, something festive." She shook her head. "Family."

"At least, you know, we have one," I said. "James didn't ever know his."

"And is he the worse for it?" She shrugged.

"Sure he is. He's had to make himself up, in a way. And I don't know anything about him, not really, because he doesn't know a lot to tell." I took a breath. "I'm scared about him meeting my folks, to tell the truth. They'll ask him all these nosy questions, the way they do."

Aunt May studied me a minute. "A word of advice, Janey. Don't pry into your young man's past. Let him be. When you're young, you believe you need to know everything about those you care for, but this is error. Did it help Kitty to know that when my father found me in bed with a friend who was visiting from Vassar, two women without their clothes, he threatened me with my life? Swearing that if he ever found me doing that again he wouldn't be responsible for himself? Did Kitty need to know that?" She removed her glasses and rubbed her eyes. "Did I need to know that her husband sicced his German shepherd on her when she tried to run away and didn't call him off until she gave in, scars on her legs still? Did I need to lie awake nights imagining that?" She pressed her palms to her knees. "A Rottweiler has moved into the neighborhood. They don't keep him penned. That is the reason I waited on the porch for you when I saw your car."

"But you wanted to, didn't you, tell each other those things?" My face felt hot to be talking about such personal matters with her.

Aunt May cleaned her glasses and put them back on. "At the time, certainly. Now, I don't know that it was wise. After all these years, I don't know." She met my eyes.

My tongue felt tied, both by the dreadfulness of the bad events she had shared, and by their echo of events in the mysteries. It seemed almost as if I were reading a new story: a hairdresser noticing bruises on a woman's neck, the judge seeing only one set of tracks in the snow. A woman mauled on her stairs by a dog. Perhaps Aunt May did live with the writer after all, a writer with long skirts and curly gray hair. And I ran the names over in my mind, the same name in two languages: *Greenwood, Boisvert.*

Aunt May stood and collected our plates and cups, as if finished with our conversation.

"Thank you," I said, "for saying Mom and Daddy can come over."

She stood at the window, looking toward the street and the car. "I'll get your wrap. It's turning colder. Put on your boots and go tend to your puppy."

22

IT APPEARED IN my mailbox, what I'd been dreading, and could not believe my mom had passed on to me: the birth announcement. Curtis Danforth Prentice, Jr., born November 14. *Danny* they'd call him. Danny Prentice who already would be locating the ability to make a smile to turn girls' heads, the business hanging there between his fat little thighs already prickling with the possibility of the future to come. Looking like his dad. His granddad. Another heartbreaker at 8 pounds 2 ounces. (How could any baby that big have been delivered by Millie Dawson who didn't look like she could carry a sparrow full term? Where had she kept him all those months?)

Mom had tucked the announcement in a lined envelope, accompanied by a real handwritten letter from her, a first.

Dear Janey,

I'm enclosing what you most likely have no desire at all to see, but you might as well know the news, since everybody else does. Plus I have to thank you for this very pretty stationery with the watercolor of a sailboat on it, which you said was done by one of your friends. Your daddy and I are glad to hear you are making friends up there.

*We ran into your old boyfriend Ralph Smalley that
you used to go with, at the Southern Fried Café last night.
You know he is working at his daddy's dealership in
Greenville. He came over and gave a great big greeting to
your daddy and I, and let it be known that his own
divorce, in case we might not have heard, was in the
works.*

*Just yesterday I ran into Millie Dawson's mom on the
street and had to look at a stack of photos as thick as a
deck of cards about Curtis Danforth Prentice, Jr., and I'm
standing there with one picture of my daughter's DOG in
my purse.*

                                        Luv u,
                                        Mom

I couldn't stop looking at the stamp-sized photo stuck on the
blue-ribboned card. I couldn't get my mind off the knowledge
that hit my chest like a sledge hammer that every baby came
with one of these: crisp white birth notice with its blue bow,
yellow Pooh bear, tiny snapshot. Or some version, some word
sent out about an arrival. Or if not a public announcement,
that every baby came with a history like this one: the Prentice
boy, the Dawson girl, that poor Daniels girl who had to leave
town. That every baby had parents. At least at the start.

By late afternoon, though, walking down the slightly icy
front stairs, bundled up in my parka and boots, heading for
downtown, I had to get my mind on more immediate matters.
Beulah, at eight months, had begun to show signs of going
into heat! Pregnancy for female puppies-in-training being the

worst possible scenario. Just as male dogs were not neutered before their selection in case they were chosen as breeders, so female puppies were not spayed until after they had completed their course. Once a gangly adolescent had to turn her attention from her person to the task of birthing, nursing and tending a litter, she had forfeited her chance to be a Companion Dog.

Today, as had been true for the last two weeks, our stroll along Church Street had become a recurrent obstacle course with all male dogs. One in particular this evening, a monster Chow-Chow whose black-tongued mouth opened at the first good sniff of her, started crowding her against the bread kiosk, and instead of tucking her between my knees—after all, you read about the male getting stuck in the female and you can't pull them apart and then the damage is done—I actually hefted her up off the ground in my arms. The Chow-Chow's person, a woman in ski pants (and ear muffs that looked as if they'd been fashioned from Chow-Chow fur) dragged him away, aggrieved. "He's *fixed*, already."

Naturally, the students with James and Pete had seen the encounter, and had to make something out of it. They reported on a study some Indian doctor, female, had done at The University of Texas involving college students and their t-shirts. It seemed that males could tell when a female ovulated by her smell. And the kids, Cubby, Wolf and Lobo as they were still calling themselves, had already been talking up this idea in their dude voices, making sniffing noises whenever some girl went by, giving thumbs up or down, making growling noises, pawing the sidewalk in their hiking boots. Smart punks. Saying to James, the teacher, "Whaddya say, is that right? You tried it out?" Now, when I'd got myself and my still-virginal girl together and joined them, one of them pointed down the street. "Hey, maybe that stud dog was just checking out Beulah's t-shirt." Lots of gross-out laughter.

After a beer and a stroll around, we all headed back to
James's place: James, Pete, the boys and I. He and Pete had
been collecting gear for taking them up into the Green
Mountains over Thanksgiving break to teach them real-life
first aid tricks. The International Living program liked their
students to be emergency-savvy, on the theory that they would
not have their parents' insurance cards, family doctor, or even
college infirmary to count on. Camping out with new friends
in unfamiliar terrain, getting mugged on their rented bikes on
the cobblestones, hiking from village to village, they needed to
master a crash course in self-sufficiency.

James had got a doctor, he explained to the boys sitting on
the floor, shoes off, who specialized in expedition medicine to
give him some pointers. In the mode of wilderness leader, he
described the makeshift solutions while Pete, his big front
teeth chewing earnestly on his lower lip while he held up different items, did the actual demonstrations: how to wash out
wounds with sandwich bags (filled with water or snowmelt),
how you could sew up wounds with dental floss, how to make
a pair of emergency glasses from duct tape (poke dozens of
tiny holes with a pin in the tape), how to stop a wound from
bleeding with a teabag (it was the tannic acid), how to use a
latex glove to give mouth-to-mouth resuscitation on a
stranger, and other stuff that apparently people died from—
when mountain climbing, wilderness hiking, or traveling overseas—because they didn't know.

Fascinating stuff for a pharmacist!

After we finished another beer and everyone devoured the
roast pork sandwiches I'd brought, Pete piled Cubby, Wolf
and Lobo in his car and took them home.

When we got Beulah settled on her towel on the kitchen
floor, I told James, "I had a little news from home."

"How about we walk on the bike path to the Dog Park?"
he suggested, starting in with the job of putting his outdoor

gear back on.

I nodded, pulling on my own sweater, parka, boots, and cap, not having any idea if that curving path out of his neighborhood was safe this late, but not worrying too much about us, mostly glad to leave Beulah locked safely inside where no Chow-Chow could leap from the bushes in the dark and try to mount her.

It actually felt grand to be out in the cold night air, just the two of us, our feet knowing the way down the path and over the bridge, the sound of the creek below us flowing under the ice. No one else was out, and the air smelled of coming snow and chimney smoke. We held gloved hands, and a raw wind stung my face. When we heard what sounded like a gunshot, I stopped dead still and grabbed the bridge railing.

"Most likely some hunter grown numb and dumb," James said.

"This close to people?"

He moved us along the path to where we could see the white-iced lake. "There's open land not too far, on the next bay. Hunters get all fall, is what it amounts to, deer hunters. Two weeks bow and arrow, couple of weeks off, then two weeks with rifle and two with muzzle-loaders. Sometimes out here you can see a deer, if it's late, running across the park."

I looked behind me as we sat close together on a bench near the rocks along the water's edge, but the woods were still. "My ex had his baby," I told James. "A boy."

He took one of my gloved hands and held it in his warm jacket pocket. After a bit he asked, "So, umm, are you okay with that?"

"The thing is, looking at that announcement which my mom for some reason needed to send me, all I could think was that even if that kid never knew a thing about his dad and me, or ever even knew the story of his dad and Millie, his mom, it doesn't matter. That's his history anyway."

"Come on, Janey—."

"James, *everybody had parents*. You had parents, whether you knew them or not."

He took my hand out of his pocket and gave it back. "Okay, all right."

I let it go. After a time, when we'd begun to feel the chill in our bones, I put my cheek against his and asked, "You want to go back and sniff my t-shirt?"

23

THE FACT OF family being an off-limits topic with James, and the fact that I'd been trying to forget mine was coming, meant it was after James got back from his Thanksgiving campout with Pete and the boys before I broke down and told him the news.

"In two weeks," I said. "They'll be here in *two weeks*."

"I don't know about that," he said, watching the French-speaking trio at the next table all in fir-trimmed parkas. We were having late afternoon lattes in a sort of European café on Church Street, at a window table, looking out at the bundled-up knees and calves of pedestrians on the sidewalk. Sitting inside had its good points after months of having coffee at the warm-weather tables outside. I liked the sound of the door opening and the swoosh of cold air, and then people taking off their coats or parkas and hanging them on racks, blowing on their hands as if they'd just come into a room with an open fire, instead of a large space filled with plants and crowded tables, two steps down as you entered.

"You have to come for the afternoon party," I said. "Aunt May says we need somebody who isn't family, somebody my daddy can talk to."

I'd left Beulah at home, loose on her leash, which she had got used to, turning away and heading for the kitchen when she saw that I was leaving. I'd taken her outside to get busy first, but she liked her backyard less and less as the snow had deepened and grown thick and crusty. She didn't like it being cold and hard under her feet; she didn't like the yellow stain, still sniffable, not sinking into the green grass the way it had in summer.

"They'll have questions," James fretted, warming his hands on his heavy mug. "Your parents."

"Don't I know." I gave him a smile, meant to convey he didn't have a clue.

"I mean, they'll *ask* me stuff." Draining the creamy caffeine, he licked the foam from his lips, then stood and fished around in his pocket for a wrinkled bill.

"They will."

He said over his shoulder as we headed out, "They'll think—*you know*."

I had to laugh. "They will. They'll think *you know* whether you come or not. They'll think *you know* just because I mentioned your name."

"Your aunt hasn't even met me." Outside, he pulled his knit cap over his ears. Snow stuck to his lashes and nose, then melted off. He'd given me a heavy wool cap, cable knit, and I covered most of my flyaway hair with it. Hair in this climate! No wonder women wore long braids or crew cuts. I'd been wearing mine longer, straight, and the bangs had grown out, making me look pretty organic not to say rural.

"Her loss," I said, slipping my hand through his arm, squeezing his parka with mine. Strolling in the holiday crowd, we saw nine white men in black tuxedos standing in a row singing madrigals in harmony, while Morgan horses pulled Hanson cabs, and miniature horses with felt reindeer horns towed toddlers in carts up the white-covered brick street. A high wind blew the snow around us in swirls, and we looked in storefronts with ornate displays of Hanukkah candles and manger scenes.

"It's going to be awkward, me being there," James groused.

"They'll think you're an improvement in my life." And I hoped against hope this was true. How could they not? But there seemed to be this small-minded loyalty to Curtis on the part of my mom especially, as if he still counted as family.

"You don't talk about them," he complained, as if all at once he wanted to hear about my kin. "I don't even know their names."

"My mom is Ida Jean; she's best friends with Madge at the bank, and big at First Methodist. My daddy is Talbot; he works at the hardware and is the very last person in South Carolina who wears a hat every time he goes out." Could I come up with anything else to say? Were they that pitiful?

Was I?

Last night, I'd baked us a chicken and sliced up the white meat with some pears and wine, really yummy on top of rice. And made the buttermilk pie I hadn't tried for him before. After Beulah was down, we'd made love on my deconstructed bed, with me rocking away in heavy socks with a sweatshirt around my neck. Cold weather sex. "What do I talk to your parents about?" He stopped on the street while we listened to some street person playing a piccolo in the falling snow.

"Anything." And I guess that was the truth, since they wouldn't be listening. They'd just be staring at Mom's aunt, wondering what was going on with her and that woman, and at my sort-of-sweetie with the straggly face hair and the look of being slightly underemployed, wishing they could turn back the clock to when they had a properly married daughter back home.

"She's a librarian, your aunt, right?" James started digging around in his parka for his gloves. The street lights had come on—so soon—and it had grown frigid.

"She's my mom's aunt, and why don't you meet her now?" Which all at once seemed a great idea. "Then she'll already know you when we come for the Christmas party. I'll ring the doorbell and just ask if I can bring something when Mom and Daddy are here. We won't go in."

He stopped and stared at me. "Then what? You tell her, 'Say hello to James.' She says, 'Hello, James.' Then what?" he looked reluctant tingeing on slightly petrified.

Suddenly cheered, I realized a bribe I hadn't even tried. "Maybe her mystery writer friend will be there," I said casually "Bert Greenwood?"

He cut his eyes in my direction with grudging interest. "No kidding? The guy who writes the Private Eyes?"

"I haven't met him myself yet—." And that was true as far as I knew.

"I get the students to read this Dutch mystery writer, he's pretty good. You get a lot of details about the country."

"We'll just stay a minute," I promised. And, happy at the idea, leaned my head back and caught melting snowflakes in my open mouth.

So that's what we did, we got in my car and drove by the university, the campus already brightly lit, a winter scene, down Black Gum past the synagogue and meeting house, to Larch, the unpaved lane which ran between two fenced cemeteries. Slowing down, I cut my light, which I'd had to turn on when the dusk deepened to twilight, and, pulling to a stop on a snow-covered stretch of yard, set the brake.

Walking across the crusted snow toward the house, I heard music, faint, drifting across the yard. "Wait," I whispered, listening. It was waltz music, coming from Aunt May's house. Quiet as hares we crossed the stretch of drifted white until, through the wide front windows, we could see a couple dancing, round and round as if at a ball. Both wearing long skirts, heads thrown back, arms on waists and outstretched to steer.

"That's your aunt?" James asked.

"The taller one. And her friend Kitty."

"That's neat."

And through the falling show, with our feet turning to ice, we stood and watched the two women dance.

Soliciting Approval

24

"I DON'T GET it," Mom said, lugging her suitcase to the bed. "I don't get the point of *Pacific View* about a thousand miles from what it's talking about. I thought you were kidding me, when you sent that postcard when you got up here? Pacific View, Vermont, ha ha. Sort of like Bay of Fundy—where is that?—South Carolina. Or Katmandu, Alabama. You know? That's what I thought." Mom had arrived at the Burlington airport in her own interpretation of my telling her people dressed down in Vermont, and that she'd need something warm.

She'd walked out of the gate in a tight pink t-shirt which said

2 GOOD
2 BE
———
4 GOTTEN

over mid-calf Capri pants in dark pink, sandals and socks, and wrapped in a huge fake-fur jacket in teddy-bear brown. Did I care how she looked, my mom? How tacky to care. And Daddy. Daddy was looking totally Elks Club (of which, however, he wasn't a member, belonging rather to the Masons, a classier lodge in his view), in a Tyrolean hat, a reversible muffler, his green car coat over a dress shirt and suspenders. I'd never met them at an airport; I'd never welcomed them to some new place. At home—well, they were just Mom and Daddy.

At the motel, Mom, unpacking her bag, hanging up her other outfits, carried on a running conversation about her friend Madge. "Her daddy, can you believe this, Janey, that fine old man whose deceased wife died two years ago, who is now in a retirement home, a nice place, has got himself a CDC. I bet you don't know what that stands for, because I didn't myself. She had to let me know the minute she heard. 'I've got myself a CDC,' she said he told her. She thought it had to do with his heart, because the connection wasn't too clear, but that's what all the old fellows want: a Constant Dinner Companion. Is that grand? Janey? Hey, Talbot. See how lucky you are?"

"Tell me this is a prank." My daddy fell back on the nearly made bed, fanning himself with a handkerchief. "You planted this, right? My own daughter, having a little sense of humor, trying to get a rise out of her old man."

Oh, shit. How could I have been expected to expurgate all the chancy items from the local newspaper? There, waving in the air, clutched in my daddy's sun-spotted hand, was a civil union announcement, on the wedding page, of two nice-looking men, attorneys, and the details of their ceremony at which a judge had presided. I felt as embarrassed as if the newly joined couple stood right here listening to him. Had he talked like that at home? And I just didn't hear him? "Daddy," I pleaded, "this is *Vermont*." Gazing out the north window of their room which faced Pacific Gas, I felt a tinge of nostalgia. A nice view that I now recalled with affection—and tried to focus on.

"Talbot," Mom scolded, "don't be having a fit. It's like kids playing bride and groom. Don't get your bowels in an uproar." Though she peered a good long time at the article herself before tucking it in her purse (for Madge?). "Her daddy's people," she continued, speaking to me as if there had been no interruption, and I would know the reference, "came from Eutaw—that's E-u-t-a-w, Alabama. I always thought that had to be an interesting place, because I imagine the same Indians that settled U-t-a-h, the state the Mormons live in, settled E-u-t-a-w." She transferred Daddy's shirts and pants to the closet, and tucked his undershorts in a drawer, carrying them carefully so they wouldn't discomfort him, being all out there in sight, his underwear.

"Two men, I never."

"Hush, Talbot, you did so ever. Remember that boy from Greenville, had been a Boy Scout?" She sat on the corner of the bed beside him, patting his knee. Speaking to me, she changed the subject. "We brought you the cutest Christmas present, and I want you to open it here, honey, because I cannot wait another minute for you to see it." She removed a gift-wrapped box from her carry-on cosmetic case—red paper and green ribbon, and handed it to me. Tearing off the wrapping, I held up six hand towels in light green, each embroidered with a dog in a space suit and a name stitched in red: BARK VADER, POOCHES LEAH, HOUND SOLO, ARTWO CANINE (R2K9), LUKE SKYWAGGER, THE EMPIRE BITES BACK. "Aren't they darling? I know you've got this little dog, so we thought . . ."

"Thanks, Mom. I really need guest towels." I tried to imagine them in my bathroom. "But you didn't need to do that." I got up and gave a hug to my mom, a tiny woman in a pink t-shirt.

"We had to get up before breakfast this morning," my daddy said, raising himself upright on the bed, making amends. "They don't fly direct up here. We had to change our plane and by that time it had got too late for breakfast. Plus,

you know what they served us on the plane? Ask your mother who had her mind set on a catered omelet with a side of
sausage. They gave us a teensy bag of pretzels. Seems they've
invented being allergic to peanuts—peanuts, did you ever?—
so they don't pass them out any more."

"I thought we could have a sandwich at my apartment, and
you could meet Beulah."

Daddy nodded up and down. "I know, the *dog*," he said.

With some regret, I packed them into my car to go to my
place. I'd been distracting myself from their talk by figuring
that actually I could have lived all year at Pacific View for the
same cost as where I was now, since naturally the motel paid
its utilities. My first cold-weather electric and gas bills had
knocked me out of my chair and left me flat on my back on
the kitchen floor hyperventilating. At home I'd paid Greenville
Water, WCRS Sewer and Trash, Piedmont Natural Gas, and
Duke Electric, every month, and the total came to less than a
single gas bill up here. No wonder the landlord with the
combed-over hair, Lavoie, had smirked when he told me: *We
pay the water; you pay the rest.*

I thought I'd be okay with bringing Mom and Daddy to my
place. It actually looked great this time of year, because you
got a bright north light out the locust-view window, and a nice
southern sun coming in the front windows. I'd grown to be as
comfortable there as in my own skin, so that I no longer
remarked on the tiny shared-with-a-dog bathroom, the
absence of a room specifically for things which took place in
bed, or the chancy encounters at all hours with the upstairs
degenerates.

But even driving down the street seemed different, through
their eyes. We passed at least half a dozen cars with bumper
stickers pertaining to the now-legal civil unions: TAKE VER-
MONT BACK, TAKE VERMONT FORWARD, TAKE VER-
MONT FROM BEHIND. Then, parking my car in the plowed

driveway and bringing them up the front steps into my apartment, I sort of lost my cool. First Daddy stopped stump-still, staring at the bare nails and hasty carpentry in the makeshift entry. "Honey, where's the rest of your place? I can't find the stairs."

I'd had it all planned. Get them settled down with pimento cheese (homemade with sweet pickle relish), on sourdough from the kiosk, with iced tea, because they drank it summer and winter, extra sweet. Then I'd spread out a fan of brochures: the excursion train to Charlotte to see the snowy countryside and get a glimpse of the village where the mysteries were set. Take a stop at the Magic Hat Brewery. Maybe ride a horse-drawn sleigh through the hilly wooded grounds at Shelburne Farms to the edge of the frost-covered lake, a blanket over our legs.

But Mom didn't warm to any of it. "Janey, Sugar, we've got trains, now don't take offense, hear, in Carolina, you may remember. And take a sleigh ride? Next you'll be wanting us to ice skate like in those old paintings, you know, with all the wintery people wrapped in scarves getting frostbite, no thank you. We want to see what there is to *see*, if you get what I mean. The shops? I have to get something for Madge that she couldn't find for herself on the internet in three seconds, at discount, something special also for Pastor Edmunds and her husband, they are very artistic people, which reminds me, by the way, I'd like to see your First Methodist, so I can report to her when I see her what the sermon is for tomorrow up here. The Second Sunday in Advent. That's going to be a topic from the Gospel of Luke about the signs in the sun and moon and stars, and the sea with the waves roaring—they like to do that one. They like to talk about the signs that the Baby is coming, or sometimes they call them *portents*."

I put away the flyers and poured myself a cup of coffee. I'd let Good Dog out of her crate, where I thought she should be when they arrived, in case they made her (as well as her person) build anxiety. Now, happy to be out and to see me again, she sat at my feet, looking up at me and then with interest at the New People—who paid her no mind whatsoever. How could they not exert even the smallest effort to make the acquaintance of my sociable companion? A word, a touch, at the most minimal, so my patient lab didn't wear herself out waiting for cues. "We'll go right by the church when we *walk Beulah* downtown," I told my mom, thanking the miracle of accidents that the town's sole Methodist Church happened to be directly on our way.

"You got TV?" Daddy asked, looking around, suddenly waking to the fact he couldn't locate one.

"No," I told him, and got up and put on the Dixie Chicks, in case the silence bothered him and having a need to hear them sing about leaving home for wide open spaces. But the phone rang, and they froze while I retrieved the cell from my parka pocket.

"THIS IS ORVILLE," a voice yelled in my ear. "JANEY? IS THAT YOU?"

"Mr. Sturgis," I answered, worried but at the same time glad to hear his voice. "Is this you?" I knew he'd got my number from my daddy when he'd called about Bayless's funeral, and I'd been calling him regularly, keeping up with everybody's medication, but he'd only called me that one time with bad news.

Mom and Daddy looked at one another, and Daddy put his hand on his chest, which looked like he was thinking of mortality.

"You got to help me out here, Janey," Mr. Sturgis said, dropping his voice to a normal range, having realized he didn't have to shout through the air from Carolina to nearly the Canadian border.

"What is it?"

"This is Orville, like I said. It's old Grady. He's taken a turn, and they've got him in the hospital, not in good condition, they're trying to figure, his old doctor, you recall, passed . . ."

"Bayless." I nodded as if he could see me. "Bayless died."

"Ex-actly. Me and Grady were pallbears. But this, now, came on sudden. He's taken a turn—Janey, what do you reckon he could've been on? He hadn't refilled anything since the funeral, near as we can find."

"Let me think. My parents are here, Mr. Sturgis, on a visit."

"Say hello, will you. That's nice. Listen, what could that old man have been taking he shouldn't have?"

I went over in my mind the combinations that Bayless had given Mr. Grady, pills he might have put on his shelf and forgot he had, then, rummaging around, thinking he needed something, maybe he'd had a right smart amount of pain, or felt short of breath, or had a sudden giving away of the knees because his doctor had died . . . I named all I could recall for Mr. Sturgis, who repeated them after me, making a clicking noise with his teeth as if counting.

"Good work," he said when I finished. "Bayless's nurse, that woman who wasn't a nurse, you recall, she's gone, gone and got herself married." He thanked me and then shouted before he hung up. "WHEN IN TARNATION ARE YOU COMING BACK DOWN HERE?"

I repeated that to Mom and Daddy, and she said, "Everybody misses you, hon, that's the truth. I hope you did the right thing running away till things cooled down. Even Millie Dawson, to get personal. I mean who else can she ask, when little Danny runs a fever?"

25

THE OUTSIDE AIR felt grand, windy and not too cold, and I'd helped bundle up Mom and Daddy against the elements. They'd talked my ear off, and my feelings had been hurt because my trusty companion had been ignored. But then what had I expected? Why did I think they would suddenly be different?

We headed toward town the back way, so Beulah could get busy before we started our walk. Mom suddenly peered at her, as if noticing Good-natured Dog for the first time, "How come you keep her locked up in that cage in there?"

"I put her in the crate when I went to get you. That's all. Most of the time she's out. But I thought, with new people—."

"Does she bite?" Mom walked a step ahead of us, glancing back as if at probable trouble.

"Mom. She's being trained to work with *a blind person*. She's gentle."

"If you say so." She clutched the railing, unsteady on the steps. "Sending me her picture, Janey, like it's some kind of member of the family. You think I'm going to get out my bill-fold and show everybody on the street *my daughter's dog*?"

Actually, I did. Not, I guess, thinking it through that some-body who never wanted to have one wasn't going to sudden-ly develop friendly feelings toward an animal just because it

happened to live with her daughter. "I thought you'd like to
see her playing in the leaves, the fall leaves."

"What the—." All at once Mom stopped dead. "God Bless
America! Is this some kind of joke?"

It took me a second to believe my eyes. BOYS it said on a
hand-lettered cardboard sign by the bare lilac bush, and
GIRLS by Beulah's spot at the base of the bare-limbed locust
tree. The upstairs guys—who earlier had been outside, puffing
and shoveling the snow from our front walk to the driveway—
had cleared a nice curving path in the backyard through the
two-foot drift to Beulah's spot, and another, ha ha, to the lilac
bush. They must have seen us come up the front steps, Larry
and his hulking roommate, Roland, must've seen Janey with
her parents and decided to have some fun.

"There's a male dog next door," I explained coolly to
Mom, inhaling a lungful of fresh air, "who sometimes comes
over here and we discourage that, because each of the
Companion Dogs has its own special place. Also Beulah is the
age to worry about *accidental pregnancies*, and I don't want
him to get her scent." Going up the driveway behind Mom
and Daddy, I stuck out my tongue and made horns at the
upstairs windows, in case the jokers were watching.

A block before Church Street, we turned north in order to
pass First United Methodist, a gray granite and red fieldstone
building with suggestions of buttresses on the side—clearly
recognizable as Methodist, though I couldn't exactly say why.
Sure enough, the sermon title, "SIGN LANGUAGE," listed
below the pastor's name in a glass-fronted display case on the
deep snow-covered churchyard, lived up to Mom's prediction,
and even cited a passage from the Gospel of Luke. "Now isn't
that smart?" Mom said, cheered. "I'll have to pass that on to
Pastor Edmunds. Didn't I tell you they'd be talking about signs
and portents this week? I did." No mention, by Mom, that
this preacher happened to be a woman, since Methodists had

had female pastors back to The Flood.

Turning at the next light, we got onto Church Street at a good location. Not too far from the classy gift shops—Symmetree, April Cornell, Frog Hollow—and not far from Apple Mountain, which sold arts and crafts by Vermont artists, and not far at all from Ben & Jerry's ice cream parlor, in which I devoutly hoped we would soon be enjoying a major dish of Cherry Garcia, in a warm, snuggy booth. "Where's your Barnes and Noble's?" Mom asked, getting out a lengthy list.

"That's way out, near a mall. There's a Border's and a local book shop here." I thought maybe she wanted to get Christmas cards.

"Which is closer? My feet don't like doing all this walking. No wonder you're wearing those shoes that look like they belong in a gym class. How do you get used to these bricks? That's like trying to do your sightseeing on the cobblestones of Savannah, which I have been to on several occasions. Though as a city it does not surpass Charleston." She leaned down, groaning, to loosen the Velcro straps on her plastic boots.

We went into the chain store, Beulah in her orange vest, and—I should have seen this coming but did not—Mom trucked right straight to the fiction shelves and pulled out every hardcover Bert Greenwood mystery, all with the title in the same rust-red lettering imposed on a snow-covered land-scape with the red brick general store in the center. "Lookit here," she said. "Not a one of them is signed. You'd think they'd have local authors sign their books, wouldn't you?" She held up *The Prisoner of Charlotte*, unsigned, to show me. "I'm going to take these with us over there tomorrow and get them signed in person, yes, I am."

At the counter, getting out a wad of what she called her "green presidents" and counting the right number, she told the clerk (a kid wearing two earrings and a lip stud) that this well-known writer here in her hands was practically family. That her own aunt happened to be his *very close friend*.

"Anything else for you?" the boy asked, slipping the books into a plastic sack.

"Rude up here, aren't they?" Mom remarked on the sidewalk, where Daddy waited for us. He looked totally out of place and clearly agitated, wearing his Tyrolean hat square on his head. And although I was glad he'd missed the lip stud, and that the lip stud had missed him, as I couldn't imagine them making allowances for one another for one second, still, I was ashamed of being ashamed of the way he looked.

Mom got most of the Christmas presents on her list at Apple Mountain. Handing me her teddy-bear fake fur coat to hold, which I let Beulah sniff lest she think I had a lapdog in my arms, Mom bought Woody Jackson cows, Warren Kimble pigs, Stephen Huneck dogs, Sabra·Field mountains—on coasters, potholders, notecards, coffee mugs. Plus she got herself a pair of black-and-white cow-print socks.

The clerk, most likely a student, admired Mom's 2 GOOD, 2 BE, 4 GOTTEN t-shirt, taking it maybe for instant messaging, and offered her a selection of cow t-shirts. But Mom decided they looked touristy. "My daughter *lives* here," she explained. "I have family here."

"Anything else for you today?" the girl asked.

Out on the sidewalk, bundled up again, Mom said, "Janey, you should have brought your Bark Vader hand towels to show her. She could use something with a little humor to it."

While she and Daddy stood in front of Ben & Jerry's, debating if it was worth standing in the line which reached out the door to find out if the ice cream really was better than Mayfield's back home, I took Beulah for a brisk walk, knowing we both needed a little exercise and a big breathing spell. "Are you all right?" I asked her. "Are they like scary people to you? Or just the people that you pass on the street that you have to keep your person from bumping into?" I gave her head a pat and longed to bury my face in her neck, but restrained myself. How was it possible to feel closer to a dog than to my own kin?

When we got back, Mom, having decided we definitely should stop for a sweet treat, started shoving her way toward the door of Ben & Jerry's, to elbow on in and snag a booth, her mind on getting out of her boots. "How do you walk on these bricks?" she moaned, two large sacks in each hand.

Suddenly Daddy, who had been warily gazing around at the Christmas crowd, came to a halt. He rasped, "Ida Jean, do you see what I see?"

"What, Talbot, what? Do not make a scene on this nice street, blocked off for pedestrians such as ourselves whose feet happen to be killing them."

"You see those two fellows down there, putting a little boy in that cart? *Two men*?

I located the males in question, youngish, in parkas and sunglasses, no hats, helping a child into a cart pulled by a miniature horse wearing red-felt reindeer horns. "Oh, Daddy," I said, "they're the boy's uncles."

And why not? Vermont had a treasure trove of uncles and aunts.

26

"PRIVATELY, BETWEEN US," Mom said, when I came to pick them up at PACIFIC VIEW for Aunt May's party, "you don't need to worry about that old gossip. Everybody asked me have you seen the baby, but tongues aren't wagging about Curtis running off the way he did anymore." Mom reached up to pat my cheek, as if giving me comforting news.

"What do you mean, have *I* seen the baby?" They were driving me bananas with these tossed-in blindsiding jabs. "They know I'm up here. Mr. Sturgis tells everybody, he said so, he tells everybody. 'Our pharmacist Janey is taking a sabbatical.'"

"It's a figure of speech, hon. They want to know there's no hard feelings, that you're interested in little Danny."

I sat on the tightly-made motel bed, looking out at the gas station. My daddy had been in the bathroom since I came. "Exactly *who* makes them think I might be interested? Maybe the same person who had to send me the birth announcement?"

"That happened to be the natural thing to do." Mom sounded defensive, like I ought to understand. "People might consider you're kin, in a way."

"No, Mom," I said, trying not to yell at her. "I am not *kin* to some infant that my one-time husband and his former cheerleader made." I wanted to curl up with Beulah on the floor and pull her blanket over my head until they were safely back in Carolina.

"Huhhh," she said, wriggling her pantyhose up her matchstick thin legs, checking the backs to see if they looked right. "I'm just saying some people might see it that way, you having been a Prentice, too, well, I know you didn't change your name, but I'm just saying, to all extents."

I tugged at my hair as if to pull it out, fresh-washed and previously looking fine. I ground my teeth. This was too much; we were heading over to Aunt May's and my mind was on how they were going to deal with the arrangement over there, plus how they'd take to James, and how he'd manage to talk to them.

Daddy at that moment came out of the motel bathroom, all dressed for the social event, and I felt actually glad to see him. He had on his white shirt and a new red silk tie with a green fir-tree motif, red suspenders, and his fall-and-winter dark suit. "How'm I looking?" he asked, his face shiny with aftershave.

"Great," I said.

Mom, not wanting the attention off her, turned slowly to let me notice *her* Sunday clothes, a red dress with gold buttons and standup collar, her Christmas dress, which showed off her figure, and red leather stilt heels, which showed off her legs and more or less put her in my altitude range when we both stood. She checked her makeup for the second time and asked me if her hair looked too "bouffant" for up here, where people didn't seem to "do" hair. "A little," I agreed, brushing it gingerly a tad flatter, more so she'd feel tended to than because it mattered.

She took the shoes off after modeling them for me, and put them in a plastic sack to carry. "I can just take my dress shoes and change at the door. I'm not going to ruin these, if you knew what they cost me, in that slush out there. People must have to do that eleventy times a day up here, check their boots and their coats every time they go in a door somewhere. I'm certainly not going to call on my blood kin wearing *snow boots*." Casting an eye on my new Banana Republic fir-green long skirt and white turtleneck sweater, she pronounced, "Young people at home hardly ever dress up any more either."

If I'd been a serious drinker, I'd have fortified myself with one of the judge's jelly glasses of bourbon, which suddenly seemed like a grand plan. In addition to the stress of the rest of it, I felt sad leaving Beulah in her crate at home—how could she understand being so unwelcome to my people?—so I wouldn't have to worry that the jokers upstairs were going to break down my door and bring in a rutting Chow-Chow just for a laugh.

James had phoned last night to mention his conclusion that it was a bad idea after all for him to go along today. "It won't work," he'd said. "It's a bad plan."

"It'll be worse if you chicken out."

"No, see, that'll give you something to talk about: me being a flake."

"James." I had suggested that he could come over and warm my bed, but he felt that as long as they were in town he shouldn't be littering my place with spoors.

"I've got *xenophobia*," he'd explained.

"Well, I've got *familophobia*."

"That would be *consanguinophobia*."

"Don't show off," I'd pleaded, "just promise you'll come. Having them here is giving me hives."

But mercifully he'd called back and given in.

Today, we picked him up at his cottage, waiting in a swirl of falling snow, the lake a platter of gray behind him, the mountains faint shapes on the skyline. Having agreed to come, he'd dressed in his best: navy shirt, gray jacket under his parka, khaki pants, his chin hair trimmed, no cap. Since I was driving, and since Mom sat up front beside me in the Honda she'd help me test-drive in the old days, James climbed in the back. He shook hands with Daddy, and then reached up front to shake hands with Mom.

"You must be glad to see Janey, Mrs. Daniels. I know she was looking forward to your visit."

"Well. We certainly are." Mom took a breath. "Jim—?"

"Uh, James." His voice cracked.

"Well, James, I'm sure you know we have *family* here in your state, who we are going to see."

Before James could answer, Daddy swiveled around to stare at Pete, who was standing in the front yard, waving his buddy goodbye. "Who's that there?"

"He's a fellow teacher," James said. "He rents the garage apartment behind my house. Janey didn't warm to the idea of my having a female teacher living right out the back door, which I'm sure you can understand."

"Certainly not," Mom said, "that wouldn't be right." She narrowed her eyes at him for thinking of it.

I watched Daddy in the rearview mirror. He looked like he was trying to follow the ins and outs of this matter of finding out that the young man still waving at our car did not necessarily have to be a matter to give his attention to. "You're a teacher, are you, boy?" he asked, as if another question was hiding beneath this one.

"Yes, sir, but primarily what I do is take students abroad, most years in the summer months. During the school term, I get them ready, I guess you could say. My country is The Netherlands; Pete, the guy who lives behind me, he takes his to Germany."

Daddy nodded, as if this was outside his area. "Good," he said.

Mom asked, "Do you speak a lot of languages, James? I

admire people who have that facility."

"I get by over there," he said, trying to meet my eyes in the mirror. "We get a lot of French practice here, being so near Montreal."

"Well, now," Mom said, "I have to admit it went out of my head, you being practically to Canada up here."

During which tooth-pulling conversation, my daddy still had part of his mind, I could tell, on the young man who lived behind James. But then, the boy was right, it wouldn't be decent, him having some girl living back there, not and be dating the daughter of Talbot H. Daniels. When you were dealing with unmarried people, which he was glad to say he did not have to do in his business with any regularity, he could see it got sticky.

Mom reached over and gave my knee a squeeze—conveying that this young man was all right, or that she'd done her best to make conversation, what could you do with men who never helped you out, or maybe she was just grabbing onto me for good luck. Because there we were at Aunt May's, at last.

A relief to everyone, by that time.

27

JAMES AND I, walking slightly ahead across the deep packed snow, could hear Mom, in her velcroed boots, griping about whoever heard of a yard this size without a sidewalk. We could hear Daddy say, "You sure this is it?"

"That was neat," I told James, letting my parka put a squeeze on his. "The bit about my not wanting a woman in your garage apartment."

"Do you?"

"You did good with them."

His voice sounded raspy with nerves. "I pretended they were the parents of one of my kids."

We rang the bell, and as soon as Aunt May opened the door, Mom dashed in, popped off her boots, slipped them into a paper sack from which she'd taken her red high heels, and passed the sack and her teddy-bear fake fur to Daddy—who stood there holding his green car coat and now her coat and the boots dripping through the paper. "Aunt May," she gushed, once she'd got herself ready. "Aren't you nice to invite your visiting family to your lovely home."

"Hello, Ida Jean, it's been a long time." Aunt May, in an elegant long wine velvet dress with an antique brooch on the shoulder, welcomed Mom and relieved Daddy of the wet boots. "Good afternoon, Janey," she said to me, giving me a brief hug before turning her attention to the men. "Talbot, I'm sure you don't remember me from the old days, but aren't you the prosperous looking merchant now." She presented her cheek to him, in the way of kissing kin, and then whisked his armload of dripping wraps into the front hall closet. "And you must be James." She took his parka and offered her hand, which wore a large ruby ring. "Janey has told me so much about you."

He looked at me, panicked, then looked back to see her smiling and finally relaxed enough to say, "I've heard, uh, about you, too."

"Come in, do, please, all of you." Aunt May took Mom's arm and escorted her into the large windowed sitting room massed with white poinsettias, and full of old things which Mom did not know the value of: rugs, books, furniture, her aunt.

"Isn't this different," Mom said, eyes wide, holding the wrapped mysteries close to her gold-buttoned chest, already slipping her feet out of her tight red shoes. "Potted flowers instead of a tree, that's so imaginative. But you always were different, Mama said."

Aunt May guided us to the half-circle of chairs arranged before a blazing fire. "Foolish of us, I'm sure, my sister and me, your mother, falling out. She sided with our daddy when he broke up the first real romance of my life. I have to admit to you, Ida Jean, I bore her a grudge even after it had all washed away."

"That's not my business, I'm sure," Mom said, lowering her eyes, as if she hadn't heard Grandmama say a zillion times that May had been prickly as a pin cushion from day one. "I just want to say how nice it is for you to have this little party for us. And I want to thank you for all the very nice things you have done for our Janey, why, without you, she wouldn't know a single soul up here in the whole state of Vermont."

Aunt May, getting us settled, said she'd made the all-white fruitcake which her own mother used to make, Mom's grand-mama—and she was sure that Ida Jean must have made it, too, from the very same recipe. She said that at first she'd thought to serve us toddies, so nice in front of a fire, but had fixed, instead, also her mother's special recipe, a floating island custard thin as buttermilk, much better with bourbon than ordinary eggnog. "I also have spiced cider," she added, "if anyone would rather?"

Mom, maybe afraid the moment would get away from her and we'd all be eating and then saying our goodbyes, poked her package toward Aunt May. "I hope it's all right, but I brought brand new copies of Mr. Greenwood's books which I personally have read all of and appreciated. I hate pushy peo-ple and I would never do that, but I wonder if I could get them autographed? If he's planning on *being here*? Mr. Greenwood?"

Aunt May took the package, crumpling the paper for the fire, and, holding up the stack of matching hardbacks, select-ed one to open. "Ah, *Hush, Sweet Charlotte*. That worked all right, didn't it? Certainly you shall have your inscriptions, Ida Jean. I don't know if Bert—you know writers, at least you know what they say, they aren't too sociable." She looked at Mom in a friendly way. "He may not join us, there's no way to soften that fact."

Mom's face fell. "Sure, I understand. He must be very busy, I know, with writing. But I already told everybody I was com-ing here to see—." She tried not to let the talk of him dwindle away.

Aunt May looked sympathetic. "I'm sure he wouldn't mind if I told you a little secret. I recently found a poem I hadn't read for years, and passed it along to Bert—librarians you know are good sources. I'm sure he'll have himself a new title soon. Here's a bit of it, Thackeray it is:

Charlotte, having seen his body
   Borne before her on a shutter,
Like a well-conducted person,
   Went on cutting bread and butter."

She smiled at Mom, her niece, like this was going to make sense to her.

Mom looked blank and then confused, and finally said, "I'm sure that will be suspenseful."

"Do you think?" Aunt May asked solemnly.

Then we heard the front door open, and felt a rush of cold air even with the warm fire, as well as a gale-size rush of anxiety, for there was Kitty, wearing a long dress of soft lavender wool, which fell loosely from a yoke on her small frame.

At the sight of her, Aunt May rose quickly and crossed the space between them. "Kitty, how lovely you look." They came into the room together, arms linked. "Ida Jean, you have here the very next thing to Bert Greenwood in the flesh, Kitty Boisvert, the author's researcher; you might even say the author's right hand."

Kitty smiled warmly, showing her slightly crooked teeth. "May, you do it all. What on earth would a writer do without a librarian to look up all those pesky details? I just paint the era to be recalled with broad brushstrokes." Running her fingers though her curly graying hair, she looked about. "Now then, of course I know Janey, and this would be her young man and aren't you nice looking. And here is—it must be—Ida Jean. Let me shake your hand. And you have to be Janey's father, wouldn't that be right? I'm honored to be included in this family event, although I know—and don't for a moment try to deny it—that you'd much rather have Bert Greenwood himself here than a poor emissary."

Mom held out her hand with the Christmas-red nails, and nodded her head up and down, being close to tears with disappointment.

The women, so much more elegantly dressed than we were, went into the kitchen to fetch us our floating island with bourbon and our all-white fruit cake. It took them a while, and we could hear their chatter, their talk about which tray to use, did we need spoons, how about the long-handled iced-tea spoons? And at first we all sat, staring at the fireplace, tongue-tied and waiting.

Finally, James got up and pretended to poke the fire, adjust the logs, and then, casually, he pulled up a chair next to my daddy, who looked startled and began to fiddle with his tie, getting the fir trees to line up straight. Daddy hadn't spoken a word so far, only perking up earlier when Aunt May made mention of *toddies* and *bourbon*. He coughed a minute to find his voice, then asked, "You been here to this house before, boy?"

James shook his head. "This is my first time. I know this area and the road with the cemeteries, and the road down below along the river, from having lived around here. This isn't that big of a town. But I never met Janey's aunt in person before. I imagine you did."

"Can't say I have. My wife's mother, quite a pistol, not the same sort as this one by a long shot, talked about her sister. They'd had a falling out. That happens, is my personal experience, in families."

"My students say that." James's arm started up as if longing to wrap itself around his neck, but resisted. He leaned back and stuck his hand in his jacket pocket, then took it out and clasped his hands behind his head. "So," he said.

Daddy, getting warmed up to the idea of a conversation, asked him, "Your folks live here? You grow up here? Your daddy a teacher, too? Seems like sometimes everybody in a family does the one thing, that's what they all do."

I bit my lip. Sort of like watching Beulah take the stairs at

Puppy Evaluation: I wanted to help out but held myself back. Then, just at the instant that James looked cornered and said, "Uh, well, sir," Aunt May and Kitty came into the room carrying trays.

"Talbot," Aunt May chided him in a gentle tone, "fine old New England families do not like to be interrogated. I know James is too nice to make a fuss, but old New England families expect you to take them at face value and not pry into their history. They're not brought up that way."

James, rescued, shot Aunt May such a look of gratitude that her cheeks flushed red. Daddy, in his turn, glowered for a second or two, like a kid being called down in class, and then, his dander up, asked, defensive, "What are you supposed to talk about then, tell me that."

Aunt May passed around the floating island laced with bourbon in tall cold glasses while Kitty passed us thin slices of the all-white fruitcake, glistening with pineapple and citron, crisp with toasted almonds. When Aunt May handed Daddy his glass, she suggested, "Tell James about how you got into the hardware business, why don't you? Young men like to hear how successful men got their start in the world."

"You want to know about that, son?" Dad took a large gulp and wiped the meringue off his top lip, then took another.

"Sure I do," James said.

"It happened like this. Back then, this would've been in '67 as I recall, I had it on my mind to be an engineer. Engineering appealed to me. Engineers made money. They built things. And people liked to ask the advice of engineers, because you had your public buildings and your roads, you had your trains and bridges, you even had your telephone pole insulators. Engineers had a lot of facets to their work, it seemed to me. But first off, we had a war, that would be your Vietnam War, and in the second place, my daddy had himself a massive coronary. And you have to put in there the fact that my girl, Ida

Jean, was not as interested in my becoming that engineer as she was with my becoming a husband."

He looked to be sure James was listening. "Now the hardware store there had been my daddy's, he wasn't the owner outright, it was just that folks called it his store, they'd say, Let's get that over to Horace's, or Let's ask Horace. So I figured that the hardware store, which in those days was the center, I mean this as true fact, the very center of the commerce of a town. In those days. Whatever you wanted, they had it at the hardware. And whatever you didn't know how to fix or look for or find or get a part for, they could do it at the hardware. So I figured, with those factors on the table and me not wanting to go to that war we had, the course of action I ought to go into was to marry Janey's mother—she wasn't that at the time, you understand—and to take my daddy's place at the hardware. That's called Runyan's now, Mr. Runyan, but you don't need to get sidetracked there."

He stopped, my daddy, and stared at James who had been listening all ears to his words. And then he stared at Aunt May in her velvet dress, and, finally, having caught his breath, asked her, "Is that what you mean? Talking my head off like a fool? Is that what you do up here in *New England*?"

Mom, who'd been fidgeting the whole time during Daddy's story, not able to open her mouth, eating tiny nibbles of her cake and trying to catch her husband's eye to hush him up, said at once to Aunt May, "This cake is absolutely delicious. A person thinks they don't like fruitcake, because of their past experience with fruitcake, the store-bought variety, and then they discover they *love* fruitcake when they taste something like this." She'd been sitting ramrod straight in her Christmas dress, her eyes narrowed, looking from one woman to the other, like she'd got some kind of notion in her bonnet, some idea she didn't like the looks of.

Aunt May asked her, "What do you think, Ida Jean, about

your daughter's use of her time up here, raising a puppy for the blind?"

"She keeps it in a cage," Mom said. "How is it supposed to be a watchdog, tell me that, locked up in a cage?"

We got fresh floating island and second pieces of cake. James put more logs on the fire. He asked what kind of wood came in a cut cord, he had an interest in woods, he said. Then he and Aunt May talked about oak and ash, birch and beech, and how each wood burned. He said he couldn't bear the notion of burning cherry, and she showed him the cherry side-board in the dining room.

Kitty sat beside Mom and asked about her women friends back home, was she going to bring them souvenirs of Vermont? Mom told her about Madge, her best friend, a loan officer at Peachland's only full-service bank, how they talked on the phone every single day at least once. How, as a matter of fact, the reason she'd wanted signed copies of Mr. Greenwood's books was so she could make a present of one of them to Madge. "We have the same exact taste in everything, and that includes reading." Kitty promised that perhaps Bert could do an extra one, inscribed to her special friend.

At the door, when we had no more excuse to linger, Aunt May helped my mom get out of her red heels, back into the plastic boots, complimenting her on her furry coat. She shook my daddy's hand twice, and thanked him for the most inter-esting conversation, as well as for coming along, since James surely did need the company of another man.

James and I lingered behind on the doorstep. "Thank you, thank you," I said, flinging my arms around both of the women.

"Our pleasure," they said together.

Then we trudged, holding gloved hands, out into the frosty, already dark, late afternoon, hearing the door close behind us.

In the still air, Mom's voice carried across the deep snow-banked yard. "Well, that was a no-brainer for sure."

"How's that, Hon?" Daddy asked, as if he didn't know the topic of the remark.

"They think we didn't see what was going on? They think we're just country cousins? It was plain as the nose on your face, Talbot. All that chummy business, you think I didn't see right through that? That woman, that little Kitty person, has flat out taken Aunt May's man away from her. That woman has plain stolen Bert Greenwood."

Avoiding Distraction

28

YELLOW TABBY APPEARED like a snake in The Garden, early in the staggering onslaught of February, the groundhog having seen her shadow and then burrowed back in for six more weeks of ice and bitter wind and back-cracking heat bills. In the house, I wore everything I owned: two tees, sweater, my good red hoodie (my constant companion), under a jacket or over my pajamas at night, plus my zip-ankle pants in the daytime. At Eastern Mountain Sports, I'd bought two pairs of thermal tights so that one always clung to my calves while the other wicked dry, and two pairs of wick-dry double-ply socks. Nobody had warned me about the intimate matter of trying, under all those layers, to remove a soggy tampon and to insert another into your *down-there* without a bloody icicle forming on your inner thigh. Last Monday, the radio had called it 8 degrees with a chill factor of minus 28. I'd called it *arctic* and sent Mom and Daddy a photo of a flock of seagulls on the snow-covered lakeshore. White on white.

Except on really frigid days, Beulah and I went for walks, her snuggy in her wool sweater and felt Companion vest. Stung by the comments of the trainer at this month's Puppy Evaluation—"You're raising a *follow* dog, not a *lead* dog."— I'd begun to trek downtown on the street with the traffic signal that chirped, birdlike, when the light changed to green. A sound supposed to encourage Big Dog Beulah to make the decision herself when to cross, with a little jiggle of the working leash from me. How on earth did blind people survive in bad weather? I imagined her in Santa Fe, all the sightless persons wearing turquoise and silver, sitting on the plaza in the warming sun against a backdrop of ochre, red and purple paintings, their trusty Companions keeping them safe from pickpockets and tourists. Would they send me pictures of Beulah? Could I even stand to think about that? Her gone?

She'd been through the bloody discharge and the onslaught of massive canines trying to mount, and had returned, older and calmer, to her eager self again. Thanks to me, she was still intact, though I was not, not in the puppy-training sense. I felt I'd been round the barn, down the garden path, in the woodshed. I'd been banging on dumpsters to create sudden, horrid noise until I suspected the Burlington police and the sanitation workers would be citing me for disturbance. I'd worked on her people reaction, noise reaction, traffic reaction, other-dog response, every day the weather permitted. Keeping in the forefront of my mind like a neon sign the trainer's bottom line: *HOW WELL DOES THE DOG DO WHEN HER RAISER IS ABSENT?*

And then appeared yellow cat. A large striped tabby, in our yard as if she lived there, sitting at the bottom of the back stairs. She'd be waiting for us in the morning when we came out back, bundled like Inuit, to get busy, and she'd be waiting for us at night, the moon already high in the dark sky, as if she believed that she was going to get fed, as if she always got fed, just as soon as she'd walked over and taken a long sniff of Beulah's spot.

Not only did she make Beulah skittish, clumsy on the steps, looking back over her shoulder in her pile of yellowed snow, but she drove the crows next door into a cawing frenzy. Therefore calling attention in the neighborhood to the fact that a certain rental property had both a dog and a cat in residence.

"Mew," she said when we appeared, me often with a cup of Green Mountain coffee sending steam into the snow-fogged air, trying to rub against my legs as if Beulah wasn't present. "Mew, mew, mew," she said in the black icy dark. "Go home, Puss," I begged, "go home." But obviously she had no home, to judge by the fact that she had no collar and the fact that no one had stapled a LOST TABBY notice to the telephone pole on our street, and that no one came out in a heavy flannel robe and winter boots calling for her.

Besides which, sending my blood pressure soaring into the low-lying sky, dandruff began to appear on Beulah's shoulders when she headed for her spot; she was *building worry*. And my own shoulders had grown flaky, too, and my own tail had started tucking under, because since the cat first started coming around, *James had vanished*. Maybe it happened just to be a correlation and not a cause, as pharmacists sometime said about feeling better when taking a certain medication, but it seemed the final awful result of the yellow cat in the snow. It made sense that orphans, such as James, might feel particularly offended by the idea of strays being unwelcome and a nuisance.

Finally, after nearly a week of tabby's unwelcome visits, I called Betty, our trusty advisor, to ask whether this was some trial that Beulah had to learn to deal with, a strange intruder in her territory, or whether I should call the Humane Society. Betty replied that if a blind person had an unwanted animal on her property that worried her dog and interfered with the dog's attention, they would send someone to take it off the property for her. But in this case, I should do it myself, for the cat's sake as well as Beulah's. "This is bad weather for any animal to be homeless."

Taking action, I picked up a HavaHeart trap early the next

morning from the Humane office, "The Place Where Friends Meet" as their sign said. Back home, I set about to cut up a whole Bell and Evans chicken and put it to soak in buttermilk, planning to cook it slow, on low, till it nearly fell of the bone. Figuring I'd have a lot of tidbits—the tail fat, the wings, the neck—to use as tempting scraps for the stray. And, for once, I didn't feel that wrench of regret that Beulah couldn't eat people food, since this meant there would be no danger of her getting herself caught in the kitty-trap before I got a chance to stop her.

Also, of course, I hoped that a fine baked chicken might persuade James to take a break from the project that had kept him busy all week, and come over for supper and to warm my bed. But he said he couldn't make it today; he'd take a blizzard-check, ha ha. "Janey, I'm picking up sandwiches from Irv's and sleeping in my clothes. I miss you, but I'd freeze it off anyway in this weather." And that felt like a major loss. I tried not to let my mind revert back to Curtis, which mostly I avoided, because that happened to be a long time and distance ago. But my ex could never get interested in sex unless I had on something he could pull up—a skirt, a nightie—by way of reassuring himself that what he had his hands on was definitely a girl, and he made clear he'd rather play pool than get near the idea of having sex with his wife wearing any kind of pants he had to pull down. So in this North Pole weather, I'd felt a rush of gratitude to be making love on a regular basis with somebody who didn't mind excavating down through three layers of various garments with legs to find the bare me.

Late in the day, having everything in place, I took Beulah's face in my hands and explained that we were getting rid of yellow cat, and, smoothing her ruffled coat, tried to believe it myself. Leaving her inside, off the leash, I headed down the stairs to the HavaHeart with a dripping strip of chicken neck. The thing worked in a tricky manner: the animal could take a step into the antechamber and nothing happened. It could take another, change its mind, back out, and nothing happened. *Hey, safe place.* But as soon as it poked a paw to snare a tad of food in the back, rigged area, the wire door came crashing down—at least so the instructions promised.

Naturally, our striped kitty, no dummy or she wouldn't have picked my back yard, when she finally moseyed into view, made a couple of forays through the open door, daintily picking her way along the wire floor, took a sniff of the chicken delight, and backed out. Once, twice. The third time, she walked around the trap to the far end and tried to paw through the wire, but she couldn't quite reach the treat. From that moment on, she didn't even look at the contraption, but stood mewing at the foot of the stairs in the cold until it turned dark, her ribs showing.

Discouraged, I was ready to forget it, but then things took a different turn. I went out after breakfast, bundled to the gills, with chicken morsel number three, a bit of wing—planning to slip it in before yellow cat came by for her morning break, when she liked to lick off the grimy snow from between her toes and groom herself before taking a stroll up the driveway. Surely, I reasoned, she couldn't resist the smell of *food* another time. But blocking my way on the steps sat the roughest of the hoody persons upstairs: Roland, the bearded goon who I was supposed to believe had cleaned up his act and presently attended classes.

"Hi, there," I said, tender wing shard in my hand, wondering if the idea was I'd have to squeeze my thighs past his raunchy bearded face to get to the yard, where the HavaHeart sat empty of animal.

"You trying to catch that cat hangs around?"

"I am." I turned sideways and scooted past him. Though I wore so many clothes, I might not have noticed if he'd copped a feel.

"You want me to wring its neck?" His bad teeth made a grin.

"Actually, no. No, really I don't."

"You won't get her that way." He gestured to my savory bait.

"Yeah?" I said. "It's Roland, right?"

"That's my name. You wondering where Larry is, Larry has got himself a visitor is the reason I am sitting on my can in the open-air Frigidaire, waiting to get into my own place."

I narrowed my eyes. "You have a better way to trap it?"

"The cat sees that chicken, she thinks, Why's nobody else around? Why aren't other kitties trying to get that? What's with the wussie dog doesn't even look at it? She figures she'll forget it. What you want, you want to put a mouse in there. She sees a mouse, she thinks the mouse got caught in the trap, she thinks I'll just sneak in there and *eat the mouse.*"

"Where am I going to get a mouse, Roland?"

"We breed them upstairs. You didn't know? Me and Larry we breed mice that the landlord doesn't give a bucket of nails we got."

"Really?" I tried to keep my ears warm and still hear. I rubbed my gloved hands together. "I don't have any."

"That's because you got the dog, though I guess she's not a real one. Larry says you're not blind, which I can see. I thought you must be, having that kind of dog leading you around."

I sat down on the step by Roland, the snow brushed away, and looked him right in the face. "Could you get me a mouse? *Today?* I have to return the air-cooled tin can tomorrow."

"Could be." He eyed me. "Could be we already got one under the sink. I hate seeing that tail stick out there. I'm kind of more disgusted than Larry about catching them. I got to get out of this place, get my own address. Sitting outside turning to a block of ice so he can screw a repeat type of the ex-wife who screwed him royal, you figure that one."

At that moment, Larry came around the side of the house, beer bottles in hand. "Hope I'm not interrupting," he said.

"What'd you do? Take her down out front? Leaving me sit here?"

"You two getting acquainted?"

"Me and her are having a talk. We need a mouse."

Larry had on a new blue parka, his hair combed and part-ed, and looked even more menacing cleaned-up than he ordi-narily did. "You going after that cat?"

"Since yesterday."

"My girlfriend says, 'That blind lady down there, she's got *pets.*'"

"Tell her thanks for noticing."

Roland wiggled his hand in the air, like he was holding something by the tail, "Dead mouse?"

"Fine, fine. I'll go check for you."

Soon the three of us were reaching through the trapdoor at the bait-end and removing the frozen greasy chicken parts and substituting a delectable lure. I couldn't make myself touch it. I gave them credit: Larry carried it down the back stairs between two wads of toilet paper, but Roland took it by the middle in his bare fingers and set it gently in place. Stepping back, I wiped my hands on my ski pants, even though I had-n't actually touched the body.

"Now what?" Larry asked, staring at the trap.

"We wait." I didn't say it with a lot of confidence. And though I spent the next hour alternately cuddling with Beulah and peering out the locust-view window, I didn't think any-thing would get tabby back inside for another try. By the time it started to flurry, I decided she might blow it off and hole up somewhere. But it was while I stood out there, a wool cap pulled down over my hair against the whipping wind, that I saw her saunter down the driveway to the cage. Sniffing the mouse through the baited end of the tunnel, she walked around and right through the open door, down the length of the wire, and, pausing to twitch her hindquarters in the way of a lion about to leap on a gazelle, pounced on the mouse. At which moment the HavaHeart door clanged shut.

Keys in hand, I ran up the outside stairs. At the top, I pounded on the door until Roland answered in just his jeans, stale hot air rushing out the doorway around him. Raising my eyes from his hairy belly, I yelled the good news. He and Larry pulled on wraps and helped me load the trap in the truck of the car, careful to put newspapers down first, and I promised them each a beer when I got back from delivering my captive to The Place Where Friends Meet. "Mew," she said, keeping a clawed paw firmly on the mouse.

So that was how come James found me an hour later, outside in my red hoodie under a sweater and parka, drinking beer on the somewhat sheltered porch between the two beefy guys who looked like escaped killers, Beulah's head in my lap, toasting our success.

"Hey, looky," Larry said. "It's your rich boy, come right up to the curb to get you. Somebody should tell him you come pick up a girl you don't sit there like a taxicab."

I could see James look and look again. I raised my bottle to him. "Hi," I called, feeling more than a little defensive.

"You come to get Janey?" Larry called out. Saying under his breath, "I had that kinda teacher."

"I got a couple now," Roland agreed.

James walked around the car and stood at the bottom of the steps. "You busy? You want to take a ride somewhere?"

Larry made a grunting noise and dropped his voice. "You got breaking news that can't wait till the girlfriend finishes her beer out here in our ice-box?"

"No," James told him, sounding angry. "Nothing special" And then, to me, "I just dropped by to say, in case you happened to be interested, that I think I found my *real dad*."

"James," I said, "wait." And tossing my bottle in an arc out onto the snow, glad Beulah had her warm sweater on, I led her carefully down the slippery steps into his car.

29

OVER EGG-SALAD sandwiches at Irv's, I said, "I thought it was the stray cat keeping you away."

"Huh?" He sat on the same side of the booth with me, and kept running his hand down my back. "I should've said something. I had my mind on surprising you. That or probably I thought I just might blow it. It was your dad did it."

"*My daddy?*"

"Yeah. The same. Talbot in hardware." He smiled and slid his fingers through my hair.

"What did he do?" I'd tried to put the whole Christmas visit out of my mind.

"Saying that at your aunt's, about how he'd meant to be an engineer but stuff came along. A lot of people would be bitter. Thinking they could've been an engineer but the breaks were against them. Going through their life feeling trapped. But then, he let it go. I forgot the words he said, but the idea was: *he let it go.* The hardware was there; he took it. And he never had regrets.

"He's worked there my whole life."

James finished his sandwich and wiped his mouth with his fingers. "Janey, listen. Don't you see, it made me think about my dad, my real dad. I mean, did he know he'd lost me? Did my mom tell him she had to give me up? Did he want to keep me, but then let go of that idea, or did he not ever know I was out there? Did he think, this is the point, did he think, like your dad said, *This is how things worked out, maybe not the way I would have asked for, but here's where I am and what I've got.* You know?"

It touched me, hearing this about my daddy, with his awful clothes and bigoted attitude. I never had half the charity in his direction that James obviously did. But what did I know about when he was young? He seemed to me to have come with Mom; I couldn't imagine him without her. I didn't even have an idea of what he might've been like—some boy who got steered into auto mechanics instead of trig, into constructing birdhouses and toolboxes in shop instead of building projects for the Science Fair in Greenville? You didn't have a glimmer of who those people who raised you used to be. Or could have been.

"He opened up to you," I said.

"Here's the hard part. I never told you about the woman who adopted me or the stuff I do know about my real people because I had too much anger to even talk about it. Okay?" He pushed away our plates, and got us into our outdoor gear again, Irv's being hot as an oven, and smelling of bacon, still, at noon, and scorched coffee, and other good diner smells.

It hurt, a little, that he'd known stuff he hadn't shared, information that he pretended all this time didn't exist. But at the same time I felt happy at the idea that finally I'd find out who he really was.

"You wanna take a drive?" he said when we'd stepped out the door into the cold.

"Sure. Beulah will be fine in the car."

"I just feel like driving. You know how you can talk when you're looking at the road and watching for traffic, and, uh, can't see the other person's face?"

"I do," I told him. Trying to get my mind around the idea

that James really had a history, like the rest of us, a past, and even had, or might have had, a family. I threw my arms around him by the car while Trusty Dog waited in the snow and he fished out his keys.

Then instantly we were sailing south along a stretch of plowed, white roadway, white mountains covered with white forests on the one hand, on the other, across the lake, the high white peaks of the Adirondacks, and not a sound, not another car in sight. Here and there a white church steeple and a cluster of white houses with white pickups and white barns, and, far away, silver bridges spanning white blanketed rivers. I could have sat, content to ride, till sundown. Once I glimpsed a hawk, perhaps circling for a snow hare, high above us.

James slowed the car as the wind blew snow off the roadside onto the windshield. Outside the window everything looked silent; inside, where it was warm, there were car sounds and our breathing.

"You okay?" James asked.

"This is beautiful."

"So, here goes." He straightened his back. "The woman who raised me, you saw her picture, her name was Norma. She told me she'd thought if she got a kid, her husband would hang around. I was—that kid. He moved out the day she brought me home."

I waited, Beulah still against my leg.

His eyes fixed on the windblown highway, he talked about her, the surrogate mother. She married right out of high school and had no skills. She tried clerking; she tried door-to-door selling. She got typing jobs and lost them. She learned dictation from a book but nobody dictated any more. "She'd say to me, 'You're not my kid, Jimmy, but I got you and I'm going to do my best by you.' She dragged her brother over to help out. Razz. Uncle Razz, she told me to call him. He'd throw me a ball once in a while; he'd give me free advice. She told me to call her *Norma*. 'You know,' she'd say, 'Norma, like Marilyn Monroe, that was her real name.' She pretended she'd taken me in to help out her sister or some friend who'd got in a jam, if anybody asked. When I shot up five feet, six feet, she couldn't stand anybody to think she was old enough to be my mom. 'He's not my boy,' she'd tell anybody who'd listen. 'Big boy like that, no way.' She'd forget if I remembered her husband or not, having invented a dozen versions of when he left. 'Jimmy,' she'd say, 'you could find him for us, I bet. I bet he'd like to hear you're half grown and all, that you turned out pretty good.'"

I pulled off my gloves and put my hand on his arm. "Oh, James, that must've been—hard."

"She spelled my name M-a-r-t-i-n. I thought that's what it was."

I put his cold fingers against my cheek.

"She got sick. Razz was the one that called me. 'Norma's in pretty bad shape, Jimmy, you better come. In case she takes a bad turn.' A couple of months later she could hardly get out of bed and the doctor started her on palliative stuff. It had eaten up her insides."

"I'm so sorry."

We pulled to one side of the road as did two cars behind us, going single file while a snowplow moved through. When both lanes were clear, James started talking again. "So at the last, I went back. I took her a Coke and a big quart paper cup of ice—she got some relief from chewing the ice—and she said, 'Sit down, Jimmy, I ought to tell you what there is to tell.' She got herself propped up. 'Get down that box on the shelf in my closet.' I hated to go in there—." He looked over at me and I nodded to let him know I was listening, then focused on the road, as a car trying to pass skidded and then righted itself. "I got down the box, it looked like a bunch of old letters and bills and junk, and mostly it was, papers she couldn't even remember what they were. She asked me to show her every one, and finally I got to this envelope that said JIMMY'S FOLKS. In her handwriting. Inside there was my original birth certificate, not the fixed-up one they do for adoptions."

"You must've freaked out."

"You can't guess if you haven't been there." He pulled the car into the empty parking lot of a rest area. "Okay if we get out a minute? Beulah's doing all right, isn't she? I'll leave the engine on."

"She's fine. I'm fine."

Outside, the two of us stood at the edge of the plowed lot, facing a stand of white-branched hardwoods, and in the distance, fir high on the slopes. He spoke in a low voice, trying to sound matter-of-fact. He had been born to a divorced woman named Lucille Freeman, no father listed. He'd asked Norma why wasn't his name Freeman, but she said the woman wanted him to have the real daddy's name: M-a-a-r-t-e-n. "Just like I saw it in The Netherlands. But Norma had changed it to the usual spelling so I wouldn't stand out in school, having a name teachers might ask about. Like she said, half the phone book that isn't Smith or Jones is Martin." He tugged off his knit cap, wiped his forehead, then pulled the cap down to his eyebrows.

I leaned against him, my head on his shoulder, so he wouldn't have to feel I was watching his face while he told me what had to be difficult to tell.

"The thing was, they got married. My real mom and dad. After they had me, *they got married*. And had *two more kids*. It like to cracked my skull open, getting that story, when I'd sort of come to terms with the breaks I'd got. How Norma'd done the best she could for me. It knocked me flat, the idea of this couple having me, then getting legal and having a couple more kids."

"How could they not have come back for you?" Or had

they tried, and couldn't locate him? He must have thought
that, too, or hoped that. Had Norma changed his name to
plain old Martin so the woman who gave him up couldn't find
him again? Did the woman cry every night, while he was
growing up with Norma, a marginal person doing her best? I
could feel his body shake against me, and it made my chest
tight thinking about both sides of it, wondering which was
worst.

He calmed himself for a minute, then went on, deep in the
story and not realizing how in the wind our feet were gradu-
ally turning to ice. "All I could think at the time she told me
was the man didn't want the baby. Maybe he wasn't sure it
was his, maybe he wanted them to start over clean. My dad.
That's who I figured didn't want to keep it. *Me*, he didn't want
to keep *me*, is what I thought."

Give away one baby and then have two more? Who could
do that? I guess I'd always thought of adoption, if I'd given it
much thought, as the big stork flying over the home of the
couple who'd been longing for a kid and leaving them one in
the cucumber patch behind the cottage under the hollyhock.
Dumb, but what did you know, what could you imagine, if
you hadn't been there?

We took turns using the rest stop, then stood a minute
more by the car, while he wrapped a muffler around his neck
and then around mine. "I went overseas that summer, after she
died, picking The Netherlands, I guess, so I could look for my
name. I never went back to Jimmy Martin. I never went back
to who I used to be. I never went back."

I was trying to take it all in.

"What your dad said over there Christmas, it really got me
to thinking."

"My daddy." That still seemed hard to believe.

"It got me to look at it in a different way."

When we'd given Beulah a little praise for being a Big Dog

and getting busy in a strange place in fresh snow, I said, "At the house you told me you thought you'd found your real dad."

He scowled, "I could've said anything at your place, seeing you hanging out on the porch with those apes."

"Come on, they helped me trap yellow cat."

"I guess."

"James—."

We had turned out of the rest stop parking lot, and were heading north, back to town, the clouds low, the wind blowing needles of snow straight at us. He kept his eyes on the road as he told me, "I looked up all the Maartens, my spelling, on the web, that's what I've been doing, and then the date they got married, if I could find that, and where they lived. You can get a lot if you know how to look. There's one Maarten married the summer after I was born, and one that married that fall. Right now I'm working on their wives' names. If I get a Lucille, maybe I'll write. Maybe I'll send an email on my *birthday*—."He made a groan. "You know, the date'll be at the top. Say, 'Greetings to you both today.'"

He turned to look at me. "Do you think?"

It made me so excited my stomach did flips. Could he really do that? It sounded to me like finding them was finding a needle in a whole Kansas-size field of hay. "When is your birthday?" I asked, to defuse it a little, and because I realized I didn't know.

"March twentieth," he said, flushing, as if he didn't like to think about that.

"Beulah's is the Ides, the fifteenth. We'll have a party."

Then, after we'd got back to the edge of town and had listened to a little radio, I asked, "James, are you scared to death about this?"

"Out of my gourd."

"But you *know* you'll find them."

30

MOM LEFT A message saying she never got around to telling me the interesting events on the phone, since in the evenings Daddy was always listening in, so she was taking this opportunity while he was at the hardware, hoping to catch me for a little private talk.

"I bet you are wearing warm clothes up there, we see on the news you are having bad weather. We didn't quite get it, that white picture you sent, but your daddy says it shows you can't tell where the land leaves off and the water begins." She made a sigh that meant she was trying to cut it short. "I know you carry that thing with you, so if you see a light blinking or something, I hope you pick up this call, because it will cut me off if I try to get into any gossip. The main thing to tell you is I'm sending you some *green presidents* to cheer you up, which I bet you need up there, that I should have sent for President's Day or Valentine's, but Mardi Gras is as good a time as ever to get yourself a nice treat.

"I don't know what to write to my blood-kin in her fine house anymore, because that is a sad situation about her and that writer. As you understand from your own recent experience, women and men do not see eye to eye on the matter of dancing with the one who brought you, if you get my meaning.

"*Would you please answer this call?*"

31

MY PRIMARY FOCUS had been getting Beulah ready for the coming Companion Dog Trials. But the sudden snow melt with its promise of clear roads lured me back to Charlotte. I hadn't got out of my mind the scene at Aunt May's house when everyone sat still as stone as the door opened, hoping for Bert Greenwood, Mom forgetting to breathe in her anticipation, and then sinking back in disappointment at the sight of the small, quite pretty historian. Or my sense that maybe the author *had* joined us after all.

Happening upon a steady stream of young cyclists pedaling single-file on the narrow back road in their bright, tight bikers' outfits, skimming along in a line which curved out of sight over a hill, caught me quite by surprise. It felt as if I'd walked straight into *Charlotte Ruse*, and, settling Beulah on the floor of the car, I went into town, thinking about that disturbing story. The Judge is having his morning coffee and listening to the locals who are arguing about whether the cyclists are vagrants who sleep in empty fields and steal apples, or whether they're athletes whose spring arrival adds a positive presence to the town. Then, just as he's about to head to work, someone remarks about what a terrible thing, old Donnelly siccing his dogs on his *own son*. The farmer looking out his back window sees two boys prop their bicycles against his big basswood tree and sneak into his barn. Angry at the notion they mean to have themselves a free night's sleep in his hayloft, he pours himself a bedtime nip of whiskey and sets the dogs on them. He's listening to the yelling and barking, when he hears a boy cry out, "Dad, it's *me*."

How much an echo of Kitty Boisvert's life that seemed.

For a long time, I stood in the parking lot of the Old Red Brick Store, eating the last of a currant scone and trying to explain it all to Beulah, while I watched the young cyclists pedal past us up the steep hill, then curve through town toward the highway heading south and the bridge to New York.

———

Dear Mom,

I'm sorry you haven't received any photos from me for a spell, but now that the roads are clear again, today seemed a fine time to take Beulah on a drive down to Charlotte. We had a nice surprise, as we pulled off onto Apple Orchard Lane to have a stroll, at the sight of scores of cyclists racing along the back road. As you can see from the pictures, they made a very colorful procession.

I know you've been blue since your visit up here before Christmas, but don't blame Aunt May. You know writers are reclusive. I'm sure that Bert Greenwood is working on a new mystery right this minute, and that she'll send it to you when it is finished, so you can be ahead of everyone in reading it.

I hope you like this note card with the watercolor of purple mountains done by my friend Sylvia. Please take care of yourselves and tell Daddy that James says hello.

Love,
Janey

32

THE APPROACHING EQUINOX brought us warmer weather, early mornings, long twilights, and gorgeous orange-red sunsets spreading across the ridged back of the Adirondacks. What the locals called mud season arrived, and we saw the yard once more: grass, crud from four months of snow on the ground, crocus, if not in our small plot greened up by Beulah's business and seeded by the wild bird food, at least in our neighbor's yard. Crocus purple and white, their stalks pale sunless shoots.

James called me in early morning from his car and I answered from the backyard where I was putting out a pie tin of water for the thirsty birds. So I was holding the phone with one hand, in just a sweater, nothing on my head, trying to set the pan down without spilling it and without letting go of Beulah's leash, all the while sniffing the air for a whiff of something blooming.

"Hey," he said.

"Hi," I said.

We'd been talking like that, checking in a lot, feeling needy and trying not to drive ourselves mad with uncertainty, as we headed for the major matters of the Future of Good Dog and the Search for the True Father.

"Pete and I are taking the kids to the hydro-electric plant," he said, "this morning. Remember, I told you? We're doing mill towns, getting the kids to understand how all the old towns were mill towns, you see it everywhere in Europe where we take them, some kind of old important mill. But the plant here's special, it's got *Sulzer Escher Wyss* turbines, and I thought, you know, maybe your dad would like to have a couple of pictures. That I'd take a camera. What do you think?"

"Absolutely." I nodded my head and smiled. Trying to imagine Talbot Daniels in the hardware store, saying to himself, *How about that Big Daddy of a German turbine, would you look at that.*

"You oughta come with us," James suggested.

"We have a bad connection here," I said, getting the water pan located where dog and person wouldn't trip over it.

"I mean it," he persisted. "Bring Beulah."

"She's lukewarm about hydroelectricity." I gave her head a rub.

"Say you were a blind person's dog in a burning building—."

"What a bad idea."

"—and you had to get your woman down the stairs, the elevators not working. They've got three flights of metal stairs in this plant. Plus the noise of the turbines. Tremendous racket. If she can handle this, the screening trials will be a piece of dog bone."

"James."

"I'm out in front of your house."

"Really? I'm out back."

I led Beulah up the driveway, cars now parking on the street again, and persuaded James to come in a minute. In the kitchen, we had some holding and nuzzling for a spell, and then I showed him the fresh coconut cake I'd made. For us to celebrate tonight—his 28th birthday and that of Year Old Dog!

"Listen, you oughta bring her and come with me," he said, looking at his watch. "I need to go."

"What exactly is a turbine?"

He made sounds that suggested he was thinking. Then attempted to explain. "Kind of, umm, a revolving wheel that goes through—." He made gestures in the air, one at waist level, the other sketching turning motions in the air.

"A huge German screw."

"Okay, you're making fun. But, no kidding, the Sulzer Escher Wyss really is beautiful. I thought maybe your dad, I mean somebody who wanted to be an engineer—."

I bent and discussed the idea of ordeal by hydro-electric plant with my faithful friend while I ran my hand down her smooth back and then rolled her over and rubbed her belly. When I put on her orange vest and working leash, she stood at attention, looking up at me with a resolute face which clearly said: *If you have a need to see heavy machines, I'll be glad to take you, just call me Escort Dog.*

James drove along the back side of the university, then down a road that connected with Riverside Drive, which followed the swift-running Winooski River. Crossing the bridge, we parked and walked along a steep street by an enormous red-brick building: the former woolen mill. At the bottom of the hill, the study-abroad students waited for us in a cheerful clump, the day bright and cloudless.

A techie who looked younger than we were, red-faced from the wind, declared himself our guide and pointed out the dam over which the river now plunged, then took us down an outside flight of stairs to show off the workings of the fish trap, which caught walleye and trout in the spring and landlocked salmon in the fall, transporting them on tank trucks upstream to their spawning grounds. We saw a display that showed the mill and the information—new only to me—that *winoskik* had been an Abenaki Indian word for *wild onion land.* I felt proud to see the way Beulah trotted carefully ahead of me down the steps without even an eyeblink of hesitation. And not at all surprised that the boys who knew us, Cubby, Wolf and Lobo, turned out to have real names (Samuel, Joshua, Joel), or that they needed to show the rest of the group that they were tight not only with teacher's girl, but also with teacher's girl's dog. While I watched, they did rounds of *Hey, hey, Beulah,* to which she responded by gazing up at each of them in recognition.

With the techie leading us, we all rode down an elevator in the main mill building which now housed the generating plant. *Elevator,* a new dog experience. A real trouper, she rode stock still by my left knee, not making a sound as our stomachs came to rest a slight beat after we did. Then James and the techie led us into the control room, where James gave his talk about how people since the beginning of settlements had located on the banks of rivers, which served as a source of power once people had learned to turn wheels with running water. "All communities," he concluded, "began as mill towns."

Then it was time for the main show, the tour of the plant's generator room three stories below. I didn't think to hesitate or turn back then, because my brain thought *heavy machines, a learning experience for Trusty Dog,* and so I jiggled the working leash, and, cautiously, followed along.

Once through the control room door, we stepped out into thin air onto a walkway made of narrow bolted strips of metal through which we glimpsed the deafening engines below. Proceeding, one canine and fifteen humans, with only the skinniest of railings to grab onto, down another steep open stairway to another walkway—the first of what appeared to be half a dozen descents in a room high as an airplane hangar. James, whose reckless idea this had been, led the group, chatting under the roar to the techie and the students, who, not seeming a bit bothered, horsed around, trying to untie each other's sneakers on the narrow metal catwalk high as a suspension bridge.

At the next set of descending metal stairs, at the foot of which a skinny platform hovered in the air directly across from the humongous engines, Beulah stopped. I shook her leash the smallest bit, but she wouldn't move. I said her name, but no way she could hear me over the pounding of the famed German turbines. I began to cry. Did blind people get to cry?

Then, in slow motion, an inch at a time, she began to *back up*. My instinct was to pick her up, to pick up my valiant dog and carry her to safety. But then I thought about Mr. Haynes, and of what he would do, if he and Blind Dog were in this frightening fix, and I knew that all he *could* do was let his Companion figure it out. So I left the leash loose, the way you were supposed to, while she backed up, one cautious step at a time. When we reached our first stairway, that is, when the first ascending step brushed her coat, she turned and started up the steps, looking *up* not *down*, with me trailing behind. James, now far below, gestured toward the control room at the next landing, and shouted, "If you're okay, I'll go on down with them. I want to get some wide-angle and zoom shots for your dad."

I nodded numbly, following along while Good Dog led us to safety.

Getting to Work

33

IT MIGHT HAVE been worry over Beulah, but most likely it was the sudden good weather that made me sick. People with pale vanilla legs and chilblains appeared all over Church Street in shorts. *Shorts. It's shorts time.* We'd had another round of late, fat-flaked flurries, but these were ignored. People, winter-blinded and slope-weary, had come to town and put on shorts. I'd washed and pressed my red hoodie and given it a spring vacation. Those who had gone to Florida had come back for Easter; those who had gone to the islands had come back for Passover. Daffodils and tulips colluded in the promise of a change of season.

And I went to the doctor.

This being common up here, where you went along through the Trojan winter without a sniffle or fever, robust, slogging along in the semi-Klondike doing lakeside jogs, and then when the air softened and grass appeared, your sinuses drained like a *fleuve*.

Trying not to swallow and cause pain, sitting on the patient's white table in the holding room, I studied the thank-yous, hand-written by small people, thumb-tacked to the wall on medical notepaper promoting Celebrex, Relafen, Prozac, Tofranil, Zantac. Out in the hall, I could hear a doctor consulting about someone in trouble, of Albuterol in the ventila-

tor, of Heparin IV, of Pravochol, and realized that just listening I'd diagnosed the patient by reflex. Realized also that I was
ready to get back where I'd be really working again, not just
reading up on clinical trials and what new drugs had gone
over the counter, but helping to figure out what to dispense
and when to dispense it. Not to mention treating *myself*
instead of sitting here out of my shoes and half out of my
clothes in some clinician's office the way I hadn't been since
high school. Coming to my senses, I reclothed my feet, scrambled into my t-shirt and grabbed my windbreaker, deciding
that what I needed I could surely pick up for myself and not
burden out-of-state Blue Cross's accountants.

It was the next week, when I could commingle and not
spread germs, and late April had brought blooms to the yards
on both sides of ours, that James found his family. We'd been
together almost constantly since the turbine trip. We'd lie on
my sofa-struggled-into-a-bed or his mat on the floor and talk
about how finding lost persons was a lot of work. How you'd
think there might be only two Maartens in the whole USA, but
there were many. How maybe *they'd* tried but then given up
on finding *him*.

We'd got into some habits. He liked to sleep next to the
wall; I liked to sleep on the outside. We'd be lying on our
backs, touching at our shoulders, hipbones and feet, talking
about his people, my dog, how little time I had left up here.
And then, when we weren't together, I'd miss that a lot. We
slept with our outside arms over our heads, fingers hooked.
And when I slept by myself, with the warmth and noises of
dreaming Beulah on her blanket on the floor, and loud party
sounds from up the street, I'd wake to find I had both arms
overhead, clasped together in the warm breeze coming in the
open window of my front room.

The morning he made his announcement, we were sitting
on the mat at his place, having waked and messed around,

then had coffee and a bowl of blueberries and strawberries. While I pulled on panties and a t-shirt, he stood and fiddled at his computer in his shorts. Then, turning, he said, "Here they are." His voice cracking with disbelief.

I stood at his shoulder and stared at what he had on the screen and then at his face. *Owen and Lucille Maarten.* Their names, small photos, an address in New Hampshire. Two children. He, a teacher; she, a former teacher. I flung my arms around him. "You found them!" *He had parents.* He truly had parents. I squeezed him till my arms gave out.

"Looks like it." Klieg lights on his face. "I waited to tell you till it all fit together, till I could be positive. But it's not only when they married and the names, but that this Lucille is the same age as the Lucille Freeman who had the baby. *Me.* I kind of went nuts, you know? Crazy and then half scared, changing my mind every other minute about contacting them. But then I just did it."

"Tell me everything." I couldn't stop staring the tiny digital images on the screen, the people who made him, the people who could have sent out a birth announcement with a little blue bow and a yellow Pooh bear. *His parents.*

"I sent them a short message, telling them my name and giving my birth date. Saying I'd like to come see them if they didn't mind; I'd like to let the other shoe drop. Was that the dumbest? The shoe drop. Christ. I might as well have said, I'd like to see how the cookie crumbles. But when you get in a state like that . . . I thought: If I don't write right now I'll never do it. So I dropped my shoe. Dumbfuck." He folded his arms around his head and grinned.

I pulled his arms down and let him bury his face on my shoulder, while I patted his back, thrilled and at the same time getting a cold stone in my stomach at the terrifying idea that maybe they wouldn't answer him. Maybe even if he did have the right people, they might have put his being born, at what surely had been the wrong time for them, out of their minds and wanted to keep it that way.

"How about we catch the ferry at Charlotte?" He sounded like the idea had just come to him. "They're running again and there's a French place on the New York side. We could have lunch and, you know, celebrate?"

"The ferry?"

"Hey, spring, cross the ice-free lake, blue sky—."

"A *ferry experience* for Big Dog?" I narrowed my eyes.

He laughed. "No challenges today. She can stay in the car. She can take a maiden pee in New York State."

It was a pleasure to be a passenger on the two-lane road and not risk a wreck at the sight of the sudden spectacular view of the Adirondacks across the lake, blue in the front range, then purple, then lavender. The rolling valley a snow-melt green as we turned onto the familiar back road, passing Ten Stones Circle Road and Apple Orchard Lane with their fruit trees, horse farms, barns and fences. And on the porches and in the driveways, and out by the livestock or walking their persons: good dogs everywhere, enjoying the fine weather.

It cheered me, to go back through Charlotte now that I had got to know the town and the country store and the people who lived here and helped the Judge. And now that I believed I knew, if not really the author, at least someone who might be the author. We passed but did not stop at The Old Red Brick Store, and I felt glad to see again the artist's clock with the Woman in the Moon face and all the objects marking the hours which figured in the mysteries. And which now gave the time as half-past turtle.

Curving down the steep road past the FERRY TO N.Y. STATE sign, James turned his head, looking giddy and still somewhat in shock, and said, "You have to go with me, if they come through. *If I get to go meet them.*"

"Of course I will. You know I will. I want to meet them the

same as you do. The only thing—I have to take Beulah to the puppy trials down in Massachusetts. You know I have to be available for that, and you know I'm going to die right on the spot, lie down flat on the ground and die, if she doesn't make it. You know that."

"We can go after," he said "If they let me come—."

At the water's edge, college students lashed the ferry to the dock, and we drove on with five other cars, two vans, and a truck, plus four couples on foot. As soon as we pulled away from the shore, a wind whipping down from Canada hit us full force and the ride turned choppy. James opened his backpack and produced a sweater for me and a windbreaker for him. We checked on Beulah through the car window, then stood at the front of the ferry with the spray covering us and the wind rocking us as we headed for the state where James grew up.

He had to lean in and raise his voice so I could hear over the motor noise. "Norma, the woman who raised me, had the whole story. She knew how Lucille had had to give me away, how she couldn't keep me, being married to an abusive man who wasn't my real father. Then how she married him, her lover, Owen Maarten, later. Right? Listen, Janey, do you think if they hadn't wanted me to know someday they'd have told her? Norma? Who couldn't do squat to earn a dime and didn't have much interest in raising a kid? Don't you see—*they left me a trail.*"

I saw how much he so totally wanted them to be glad to hear from him and claim him, and to make amends for leaving him outside their family all these years. And my eyes stung not just from the wind blowing the churning water on my face. They had to want him; they had to.

We drove off the ferry, up a rocky ramp, onto a neighborhood street—to discover that the French place he remembered had changed to a lakeside café that was called—the Vermont influence—Lakeside Café. Parking the car, I led Beulah to a secluded spot by a shrub near the curb and invited her to get busy. Then, deciding the café looked as if it would welcome her without a vest, we walked through the bright white and blue nautical interior, which had life preservers on the walls and the rocking feeling of being on floating piers, and sat with her at an outside table on the windblown deck. Putting her on the loose leash so she could stretch her legs, we each ordered a beer, and, damp and tired, left our menus unopened.

"Here's to—them," James toasted, lifting his bottle, his face glassy with hope.

"To them." I clicked my bottle against his.

"The last time I was in this cafe," he said, his voice wobbly, "in the place it used to be, anyway, I was *Jimmy Martin.*"

34

MOM CALLED WITH hurt feelings, to say she hadn't got a card, not to mention flowers, from her only daughter for Easter and her only daughter had not even asked about the annual Easter potluck lunch at First Methodist.

"Sorry," I told her. "It's been—hectic. Mostly all I did the last month was get Beulah ready for her last Puppy Evaluation before the Training Trials." I couldn't go into the hydro-electric ordeal. I couldn't mention anything about James's hope that he had found real parents. And I guess it was the first time, or at least noticing it was the first, that there wasn't much of anything at all I'd been doing that I could tell my folks about.

"Uh, huh," she said, not about to spend time on my dog. "Let me tell you, since you forgot to ask, about the ambrosia I fixed, as my contribution to potluck, which in some cases, I have to say, even for church people who ought to give the occasion some care, is too much luck and not enough pot. My ambrosia, as I don't have to remind you, is a legend. I could have made twice as much and not brought home a spoon of it. Isn't that right, Talbot?"

Daddy, on the other phone, agreed. "Your mother's a legend."

"You get that instant pistachio pudding—which is not just

on any shelf, let me tell you—the canned chunky pineapple and canned crushed pineapple, see you have different textures here, and shredded coconut, which you used to could get without sweeteners, but now you have to allow, and chopped pecans and those little marshmallows. I don't like the colored ones. You stir in Reddi-wip, and then garnish it with maraschino cherries. I didn't write you about that, honey, if you want the truth, on those nice water-color note cards you sent me, because I didn't know how to spell *maraschino*."

Daddy chimed in, "Your mother is just saying that, the actual truth is she wanted to talk to our daughter, you, today. She had the blues, not hearing from you."

Mom admitted it. "We don't hear from you and we don't hear from you, and people are asking about you, and if you're going to let Millie and the baby stay in that house that was yours, and what Curtis plans to do for you. And I have to say you haven't shared this information with your own mother. Plus they had Danny's christening in our very own church, now how many tongues do you think wagged over that?"

"Mom." Where my life was headed after Beulah went on to a blind person or didn't, I hadn't a clue about or even minimal interest in at this minute, with her standing by my chair, and both of us wanting to get out into the bright sun and romp about. Past that, I couldn't get my mind around it. Maybe I'd sleep in my car or rent a room over the garage behind Curtis's mom's house. That would give the town something to talk about. "Mom, I don't know."

Daddy coughed, to let me know he intended to get a word in. "Tell that boy of yours I enjoyed the photographs of the machines in the water-power plant. I bet they make a racket will take your head off, something that big. I put them up in the hardware on the bulletin, they're of interest to customers. I put a little sign under them, YOUR RUN OF THE MILL TURBINES, because that's a figure of speech, you see, but here they are doing that exact thing. I mean they used to. Run the mill."

"James will like hearing that," I told him.

"Well, sweetie, on that topic," Mom said, "you could move that boy along a bit, somebody like that, a studious type, they need a little prod sometimes to get themselves to notice that a certain marriageable person is about to get away from them."

"He's taking students abroad this summer, Mom."

"Well, we've got fall down here, remember. Tell him to come see our fall. Just because we don't put it in the paper and call our leaves *foliage*."

35

BEULAH AND I went to the Dog Park every afternoon now that spring had truly come. Old enough to understand that the umbilical leash meant she could frolic about with the other dogs, she made her own canine social on the newly-mowed hillside near the lakefront. Sometimes puppies came up to her, walking under her like a stepladder, the way she'd once done with bigger dogs. Today, in addition to the usual labs and shepherds, a collection of other dogs leapt in the air after their watermelon-slice Frisbees or played, as Beulah did, fetching yellow tennis balls—a wolfhound, a boxer, a Bernese Mountain Dog much like the one James had borrowed the afternoon we met, a corgi, a cairn terrier, a pair of Jack Russells. James had got an email from the woman, Lucille, that said: *We would be glad to see you, James.* And gave him a choice of two dates in May, both Saturdays. After getting me to promise that of course I'd go with him, that I wanted to be there when he met them, he accepted the later date—an afternoon which fell exactly a week after Beulah's Companion Dog Trials. We could hardly talk about either event when we were together for being so anxious we were climbing out of our skins. Sometimes, we'd be walking downtown—musicians playing at both ends of Church Street, students in cutoffs and tees and headbands flocking together to celebrate the late sunset and signs of summer—holding hands, in a daze. I'd look at him and mimic somebody going nuts; he'd look at me and roll his eyes and stick out his tongue. Sometimes we leaned our foreheads together and groaned, "Uhhhhh."

Then, in a happy surprise, Aunt May called to say that now the warm weather had come, she wanted to make sure to see me before I left. "Janey, Kitty and I feared we would look up one day in May, and here it is in fact such a day, and find you had slipped out of town as swiftly as you slipped in. And I not too welcoming, I'm afraid, on your arrival. For various reclusive reasons, no doubt. At any rate, we do so want you to come for a last supper, please do not read anything religious in that unfortunate phrase, with us. Is this Friday too sudden for you?"

"That would be wonderful," I told her. "May I bring James?"

Aunt May coughed. "I took the liberty of calling him when I could not reach you. He accepted at once and said he had news for us. I didn't pry."

"Yes," I said. "He does, but I'll let him tell you."

"Certainly, you should."

Dressing up for Aunt May's very welcome supper, with its prospect of good food and some much-needed talk, James trimmed his face-hair, left off his headgear, and put on his best blue-striped dress shirt, and sort-of-ironed khakis. I dug out a long cotton skirt, an old one, cut on the bias, a southern pale rose, and wore it with a pale new t-shirt, which felt festive as a ballgown after bluejeans all winter. And my clean hair rejoiced to blow about in the warm air, with nothing smashing it down. We brought a sack of fresh vine-ripened tomatoes, the stems still on. I tried to find a greengrocer in the market where I bought them, to ask him where they came from this time of year, fragrant as if fresh from the garden.

The black locust in Aunt May's yard had leafed out,

though it did not yet have the thick white flowers which smelled like gardenias. I'd be gone when they were blooming. She had a large round iris bed in the front lawn, last seen buried in snow—purples, browns, golds, like a Japanese painting. I parked on the edge of the yard, off the street, and got out of the car with our sack of tomatoes and Beulah on her long leash. I had the idea we'd walk her down the street between the two cemeteries a bit, then let her find a spot to get busy, before closing her in the car.

Aunt May stood on the front steps, and I stopped, leash in one hand, tomatoes in the other. I didn't want her to think I meant to bring the dog inside. So I turned, deciding to put Beulah back in the car, just as James said, "Your aunt has a *gun.*" I couldn't believe I heard him right.

But indeed there stood Aunt May with what looked to be a pistol in her hand, pointing it at a dog. The dog—it was a Rottweiler—bending over something on the ground, pawing it. *Kitty.*

I quickly pulled the leash from Beulah's neck and told her to stay. "Don't let her move, James. Stand with her." Even as I spoke, I began to run across the lawn, doubling the heavy leather in my hand.

Coming closer, I could see that Kitty must have tripped on a tree root—she lay facedown, cut peonies flung in all directions around her. The dog's scissoring teeth tore at the shoulder of her cotton sweater as I came near. "Back," I yelled at him. "Back, Fritz. *BACK, FRITZ.*" In my fear, punctuating my words by snapping the leather in the black attack dog's face. I didn't try to pull him off Kitty or look at her, afraid he would turn on her again. When he stopped, his small red eyes watching me, his front paws still on her, I advanced, slapping the ground in front of him with the doubled-up leash the way you saw lion trainers hit the ground with their whips to make the giant cats back up. All the while Kitty lay still, not making a whimper, not allowing herself to stir. Finally, when the dog, its panting mouth open, began to turn away and then run toward the trees at the back of the lot, I hurled the leash after him. Tearing off a sandal, I threw that at him, too.

First I helped Kitty to her feet, locating her glasses and gathering the cut blooms, then I turned to see about Beulah. Stalwart, she stood motionless beside James, but her ears and tail were up, as if she longed to come to my side. I retrieved the leash and tossed it to him, so that he could put her safely in the car, then walked Kitty to the front door where Aunt May stood, still holding the gun. "If you hadn't shown up when you did, I'd have shot it," she said, her hand steady.

Inside, Kitty wiped her face, streaked with grass and dirt, a skinned spot on one temple, and accepted a glass of bourbon from Aunt May, who was still breathing heavily. Pulling off the torn sweater, the small woman poked at a tear in the sleeve of her light green dress, then, taking a sizeable swallow, she made a shaky smile and asked me, "However did you come up with *Fritz*?"

By then James had come in and joined me on the wide sofa. I felt sick with relief that Kitty was all right, and, trying to slow my racing heart, explained, "Our dogs learn to answer to their names, that's how you—get their attention. I thought maybe any name, just the tone of a name, would do it. I didn't know what else to try."

Aunt May took my face in her cold hands. "How resourceful you were," she said. "I should have shot it." She folded her arms across her chest.

"Come on, Bertie," Kitty snapped, "put it in the story."

"In the story," Aunt May raised her voice, "the hairdresser *shoots the dog*. And I have the job of defending her."

Kitty laughed and drained her glass.

James and I stared at one another.

"*You?*" he asked.

Aunt May shrugged and sat down heavily. "You two must have guessed," she said.

"I thought it was Kitty. *Boisvert . . . Greenwood*," I said.

"Well, yes." She clasped her hands, looking amused. "I did appropriate her last name, it's true. And my first name is Bertha. Bertha Mayfield Mason, what could I do with that?"

Staring at my aunt, *Bert Greenwood*, it fell into place, as if I'd known it all along. She, the Judge, observing, putting it all together; borrowing from Kitty the bourbon, the dreadful dog attack, the wise librarian with the curly gray hair.

"Let's not forget supper," Aunt May said, rising and leading us into the kitchen. "Drama is no substitute for food." Glancing about, as if to reconstruct where she'd been when she heard Kitty cry out, she peered in the oven where she said a cut-up chicken roasted, and checked on the vegetables. She let James pour her, and us, a glass of wine.

Trying to collect myself, I read a newspaper item pinned on their bulletin board:

KENYA: MARRIED WOMEN SEPARATE. An 80-year-old woman in a Western tribe has divorced her young wife because of "cruelty and violence." Some tribes allow women to marry when an elderly widow has not had a son and one is needed to perpetuate the family line.

Someone had written in the margin: *Not very civil union.*

———

After a bit, we took our glasses to the table, set with four candles, yellow placemats, and a fluted vase with a stem of forsythia in the center. James and I sat on one side, the women on the other. The baked chicken was delicious, and we had roasted new potatoes, asparagus with the stems half-peeled, and curried squash in a kind of soufflé. *Spring! Home-cooked food*! We didn't say a blessing, but we raised our glasses to one another, and when Aunt May took Kitty's hand, James reached out for mine.

We had the salad course after, with the tomatoes, in a lemony dressing. Kitty, putting down her fork, spoke to James, her voice still a little shaky. "Janey has done her part, saving me not only from a marauding dog but also from a wild woman with a contraband gun . . ."

Aunt May reminded her dryly. "You don't need a gun license in Vermont."

". . . Now we understand you have something to tell us."

James looked from one to the other of the women. The terror outside had quite taken the edge off his excitement, but he flushed to be able to give them his news. "I found—my real dad and mom. We're going—going to *meet them*. In New Hampshire, in a couple of weeks."

"Is that good, then, do you think?" Aunt May asked. "Not to be unfeeling, and certainly excepting Janey, but some of us might like to have let ours stay lost."

Kitty looked at me and then at him. "May wishes she'd been an orphan on a doorstep because she had that big southern family. She does not, however, wish she'd been raised by dingbats or crazies? Do you, Bertie?"

Aunt May shook her head. "I was out of line, James. Please. I'm still in a bit of shock, seeing that damn dog leap on her."

Kitty said, "Tell us about them, James, these people of yours. Do they know you're coming?

He told the whole story, then, not all of it, naturally, but enough so that they could see how the moment he brought up the faces of Lucille and Owen on the computer screen, he felt his hopes had been answered.

Back in the room with the bay windows, Aunt May was

bringing us warm pudding with plum sauce for our dessert. But I had grown too antsy to sit a moment longer. What if Beulah thought, now, that every time I told her to "stay" it meant a dangerous dog was attacking? What if she'd lost her trust? What if she waited out there in the car thinking her person was never coming back? "Excuse me," I said to the women, "after that awful Rottweiler, I have to, I just have to, be sure Beulah's all right."

"Oh, for God's sake, May," Kitty protested, "do let Janey bring the puppy in. I quite forgot about it outside."

Aunt May set the plates down and looked toward the dark window. "Certainly," she said, after a minute, "certainly your animal ought not to be out there alone."

I ran to the car, nearly tripping myself, and covered her with hugs while I took her from the front seat floor and calmed her trembling with a little stroking.

Together, we walked through the front door of the large house with its dark wood floors, its scattered rugs and musty-book smell unfamiliar to her, moving down the long hall into the light windowed room where everyone waited. In the middle of the room, she stopped, looked all about, and then slowly approached Kitty. After a slight hesitation, she put her face on Kitty's knee.

"She was afraid for you," I said.

"Oh, my." Kitty spoke softly, patting Beulah's head. "It's not your fault, dear," she said. "We can tell the good guys from the bad guys."

36

LARRY AND ROLAND made a dozen trips down the back stairs and up the front stairs, loading their gear into Larry's car and Roland's truck. Their lease didn't expire till June 1, the same as mine, but they'd decided they had to either split or kill each other. Larry got the girl he'd been screwing upstairs to let him move in with her, on a sort of we'll-see basis, and Roland pressured his younger brother to let him have a room till the end of summer. Larry left me a goodbye sign on the now leafy, blooming lilac bush: LARRY WAS HERE. I gave them each a Magic Hat and waved them goodbye. And then it did seem time for me to go, too.

I'd rented a place back home—sight unseen since naturally I knew the area—equidistant from my former home now inhabited by Baby Danny Prentice and his parents, and Mom and Daddy's house. The realtor said certainly, since it was a single-family dwelling, I could have a pet, but that would require a larger property deposit since it had been their experience that pets tended to depreciate the value of a rental. I didn't intend to jinx in any way a single thing about the Companion Dog Trials by socking down a guarantee on a place that didn't allow dogs.

I told James that no matter what happened with Beulah, of course I'd go with him to see Lucille and Owen, which is what we'd been calling the couple, his natural parents, anything else seeming too familiar and too hopeful for him to say. And I guess I was truly as thrilled as he was about making the trip, and the possibility that he'd end up with a real family. And as terrified. Because he had to work with his kids and couldn't go with me to the Trials, he'd printed out pages of detailed roadmaps of Massachusetts, and given me the exit number of two places with both coffee and public bathrooms, since the state of Vermont did not allow any commercial signs on the highway. I didn't have the heart to tell him that I'd got a card from the Companions giving us the route, the exit number, and street directions from there, in case we'd set our hearts on watching our good dogs run through the trials.

I'd read the Companion Dog Trials Information Guide until I got cold chills just looking at the gray cover. It warned: *Sometimes a dog will do well with its person present but will not have enough confidence to do well when its person is absent.* Confidence. That was the key word. Confidence in the face of loud noises and strange objects and scary people and heavy traffic and other dogs. Confidence on country roads with no sidewalks and on crowded city streets and public buses, trains and escalators. *The confident dog responds well to different handlers. (S)he accepts kennel life.* Kennel! I started leaving her part of every day in her crate, but that wasn't the same as being all the time enclosed in a metal cage while she learned to be a true companion dog. How could she stand it? How could I stand even thinking about it? Here she could follow me into the kitchen while we conversed. She could lie at my feet when I was reading, or flop on her blanket by the window when it was bedtime. And always get a nighttime body rub and full-body hug from me, and always hear my voice telling her *good girl, good dog, beautiful Big Dog Beulah.*

I imagined the new regime, the trainer shouting into the

kennel at dawn: "Up you canines and make it snappy, dry food on the quarter hour, no snuffling around or griping, look alert and ready to work, today we're teaching you how not to run your sightless persons into mailboxes and telephone poles."

The night before the screening, I had sweat running down my armpits and into my socks and the trots and sick-stomach syndrome. I cried and then gave Beulah and me the Maximally Miscegenic shower and ate my bowl of Ben & Jerry's Cherry Garcia on the floor while she ate her nibble of kibble. Finally falling asleep in my bathrobe, my head nestled between her paws.

The Companions were taking the dogs (four from our group) to the trials in the van without us, which meant I'd go down alone, and, if Beulah failed the drill, I'd come back alone and pick her up at the Puppy Social location. I'd made a motel reservation in Massachusetts, thinking I'd like to have the night there with her, if she didn't make it, and there to blubber till morning if she did. And then cancelled it. If she didn't qualify, she'd have to go home in the van that brought her; if she did, she'd stay. So whatever happened, I'd do the trip in a day, leaving before seven in the morning, getting home after nine at night. Heartsick, either way it went.

I was a wreck, trying to drive the speed limit on the highway, and pulled over into a rest area, to have a nervous pee and, on impulse buy an ice-cold Coke, probably the first ever since I got my period at thirteen. Caffeine, sugar, calories with each bubbly swallow. I might also have dug the coins out of my beat-up quilted cow-purse for a double-almond Hershey, if one had been available, and found even thinking of the milk-chocolate a boost.

The directions were good, and I turned in at the Companion Dog Kennels forty-five minutes ahead of the start of the trials. There were already Companions there as well as trainers and instructors. The women in kennel t-shirts had a sort of tenseness about them—small wonder, considering how hard they worked to get a couple dozen dogs a year ready to be matched up, half of them anyway, the lucky half, with some blind person with whom they made a good fit in personality, energy, and living situations.

One other person from our Puppy Social was there, and though I hadn't warmed to him before, had thought him arrogant and cocky, of course I now greeted him like my next of kin. For one thing, I didn't know anyone else who had a dog in the trials. For another, I knew he wouldn't be here, all the way down at this kennel in western Mass., if his gut wasn't also turning like a butter churn.

"I'm going nuts," I told him.

"I want to keep him and I don't, you know?" He looked a mess.

"I know."

"You want a Coke?"

"You bet. My mouth's dry as the Sahara." I located a grateful glance. "My name's Janey. I'm Beulah's person." I gave him a clammy hand to shake, having forgotten his name if I ever heard it. You could remember the dogs—his huge golden lab trying to hump every puppy in sight—but not the people.

"Vic," he said. "V, same as Vijay. How about that?"

By the time they were to start, we'd stoked up on our colas and the chocolate-chip cookies set out for the crowd, and said hellos to Betty and the other Companions from home who had brought our dogs down in the van. We waved to Patsy and Deirdre, the pair who had conducted our Puppy Evaluations, which felt like greeting Algebra teachers who'd just given you a grade of C for the second straight semester. I spotted Naomi, the curious black lab, and Tory, though not his person, the nice woman who'd had to watch him fail to climb the stairs and not quite snap to attention when he heard his name.

Rhonda, the one who puddled, and Sherry, the shy one, had dropped out.

"You think they're all in the kennels now?" I asked, as we decided it was time to get out of sight: a requirement for those who had dogs under consideration. If we gave *any* signal or let ourselves be seen or smelled, then the dogs would immediately be cut from consideration.

Vic blew his nose and we hunkered down behind a hedge along the open field where the judging would take place. "Vijay doesn't like being cooped up," he said, looking stricken.

When the handlers brought them out onto the field, I bent double. "I'm going to be sick."

"Naw," he said, "that won't help."

"I'm going to walk around the parking lot, then."

"I'll wave when they start."

If I didn't lose count, I trotted past my car forty-two times before I heard what sounded like dogs and saw Vic, a husky guy with a lot of gut, semaphore his hands back and forth.

Joining him in our hidden location, I saw what looked like two dozen dogs gathered on the edge of the field, all at attention, each on a leash. At first I couldn't see Beulah and then I did, in the middle of the group, looking around (*Where is my person?*), but standing straight in her working vest. I couldn't tell if she recognized her Puppy Social playmates, and I spotted Vijay but couldn't find Naomi or Tory. There were at least three golden retrievers who looked so much like Edgar, poor Edgar, who would have been a star if not for his windpipe. Not your fault, your ancestors.

After about six dogs had been tested, I started clawing at Vic's shirt, which had got wringing wet. He said he was out of here after Vijay's turn, going to go down the road and get a six-pack and come back for the verdict. But in fact he didn't leave, and Vijay did great: confident, in control, when they

opened the umbrella in his face, he charged right at it. When
someone in a Halloween fright suit with wild white hair and
fangs leapt out at him, he stood his ground. Waiting with the
crowd of dogs, he hadn't jumped a single one. I still wouldn't
have called him lovable—I could see he thought he was Top
Dog, but that counted for a lot. I squeezed Vic's arm while his
lab was out there, and by the end he had tears covering his
jowly red face. "*Good boy*," he growled, wiping his eyes with
his sopping shirtsleeve.

Naomi came next, and when they brought out a giant
inflated cat she went right over to it and poked its nose. She
sniffed the groin of the scary person in the white wig, and
seemed her old nosy, cheerful self, even giving a little tail-wag,
though I didn't know if that was okay or not. But when they
walked her up and down, snapped her to attention, then had
her stay while they walked the length of the field away from
her, her attention didn't hold. *What's going on here?* she
seemed to say. *What's that over there? What do I smell?* And
I understood why her person hadn't been able to watch.

Then, after two other dogs, they called, "Beulah." The
eleventh dog. Things got dead quiet in my head, and my eyes
faded in and out so that I kept forgetting to breathe. They
made awful noises—banging two pans together, first on one
side of her head and then on the other. And I imagined I could
see her think: *My person is banging the dumpsters.* And then
they led her up a flight of open stairs to the top of a wooden
viewing tower and down again, and she did them as easily as
our steps at home—heading down to do her business, not
minding the guys upstairs. And every time they said her name,
"Beulah," she attended, and she did all her commands just
right. But in between their instructions, I could see her turn
her head sometimes ever so slightly (*Where is my person?
Where is my person?*), and I could see small signs of worry ruff
her coat. Vic rubbed the back of my neck with his huge sweaty

hand as we peered through the hedge at my good dog.

And then, suddenly, while she walked briskly alongside her instructor, they snapped the large black umbrella open in her face. Slowly, ever so slowly—exactly the way she'd done at the hydro-electric plant—she began to back up with the handler at her side, never taking her eyes from the unexpected object, *moving her person away from danger.*

"Oh, Beulah," I whispered, sinking to my knees in relief and hope, "Oh, Baby, that's the way."

37

WE'D SET THE time for mid-afternoon, so that if they didn't feed us anything, if the woman met us at the door and whispered, "I'm going to tell him you're my cousin's stepson," and we were back on the road in eleven minutes, there would still be daylight for the trip back home.

"You called her?" I asked, as we turned south at the Hanover Inn onto a state road. It wasn't really a question.

"I told you all that." He had both hands on the wheel, concentrating like he was driving the Indy 500, not another car in sight. He'd worn a white dress shirt, sleeves rolled, and jeans. Long-lost son clothes.

"Tell me again." I wasn't too calm myself.

"I called her, Lucille, after I got her email. I told her I'd been born to Lucille Freeman, and gave her my birth date, which I'd done when I wrote. She asked me, 'What name do you go by?'" And I told her Maarten. 'All right,' she said, and asked if I had a pen so she could give me directions to their house."

I had nerves, wanting this for him in the worst way, but scared of the reception we might get. How could people let you go, and go on about their lives as if you'd never happened? I'd worn my pale southern tee over cropped pants, and my armpits were as damp as if I was back at another puppy trial, and I guess I was, in a way.

"That was Dartmouth back there, where I didn't go."

I laughed. "I didn't either."

"I mean, you know, I thought about it—."

Fifteen miles down the two-lane road, he turned left on a street with a large brick corner house that had a FOR SALE sign in the yard. He checked his notes. "Six blocks from here on the right, it says." He slowed the car to a crawl, creeping through intersections. As we got closer, he rubbed the top of his head, as if to make sure it was still there. "It's the next block," he said. "Whoa. I don't know anything to say but 'Hey, I'm your kid.' That's going to freak them out."

"They know that, James. Don't they?"

"I guess, yeah. Hell, I don't know." He stopped the car at a yellow house, studied the page of directions one more time. "This is it." He stared at me in panic. "*Janey.*"

"What?"

"If I freeze up, help me out."

"Sure," I promised, not having any more idea than he what to say.

The woman who opened the door, small, neat, her brown hair graying, studied us a minute, then showed us in. "So you are James," she said, making a small smile. "Yes, I can see that."

"This is . . ." He turned, almost bumping into me.

"I'm Janey Daniels." I held out my hand.

"A southern voice?" she asked.

"I'm from Carolina, South Carolina."

"All right," she said. She seemed quite reserved, quite contained, as if she did not expect things to be easy. "Come into the kitchen. I would like to tell you some of it before Owen comes home. Will you wait for refreshments? Do you need a bathroom?"

"We're okay," James said, and I nodded.

She waved us onto kitchen chairs in a sunny room with windows looking out on a backyard with three bird feeders. She stood, wearing a neat shirtwaist dress, pressing her palms together. "I had a youthful marriage to an abusive man. All right? Owen and I met; we were both teachers at that time. Not here, not in this state." She glanced at James. "You know that."

He nodded, and swallowed.

The woman, Lucille, continued, her voice low. "I got pregnant. If my husband had found out, I could never have got free. I had to leave before it was apparent, and hide out. He was the type of man, if he'd learned I was pregnant, would have become violent. Perhaps you've known others like that. He'd had a vasectomy, to ensure I had no reason for birth control."

James seemed about to ask something, half rising in his chair, but at that moment the front door opened, and we heard a man's voice. "Lu," he called, "you in there?"

"I'm in the kitchen, Owen." She waited, composed, pressing her lips together. When he came into the room, a tall man, he looked familiar, as if I'd seen him before. It took me a minute, while he crossed the room to kiss his wife, to take in the combed-back dark hair, the blue eyes.

"This is James Maarten," she said to him. "And his friend Janey Daniels, who is from South Carolina." To us, she explained that Owen put in time at the high school on Saturday afternoons, helping with student science projects.

"Maarten?" The man reached out his hand when James rose. "Well, I certainly can tell that without needing to be told. Now you're too young to be one of my brother Reg's boys; I expect you must be my Cousin Andy's boy. Stand up here and let me see, I swear."

And the resemblance between the two of them took my breath.

"Owen," the woman said, "he's *our* boy."

The man flung his arms around James and a low crying sound came from his throat. "It's him?" He held James out and looked at him, his eyes wet. "It's the answer to a prayer. You'd be twenty-eight, isn't that so? Sure, it is. I can tell you the day in March." He wiped his eyes. "Lu, you must've fainted when you saw him at the door."

She smiled slightly. "I'm not a fainter, Owen, but I have to admit it knocked the wind clear out of me, how he favors you."

Owen seated us all at the table, and they served us homemade, cream-cheese frosted carrot cake and filtered decaf coffee. Although they asked if we'd like something else, it was clear the cake had been prepared just for us, as the kitchen was still warm and smelled of spices.

Owen kept looking at James as if he couldn't yet believe his eyes. "I wanted to kill that man, her husband, that John Freeman. But Lu said if we gave up the baby, she could get her divorce. She and I had been together while she was married. You might as well know that. We'd found ourselves in love and didn't use precautions, though now I see you here, I'm glad for our carelessness."

James put down his fork, finding it hard to eat. "I can understand that, sir."

"Tell me now, how was it you found us?"

James explained that the woman who raised him had given him their name, at the last. He looked away, and a sigh escaped him—maybe something about all those other years or maybe no longer holding his breath. "These days," he said, as if he'd waited for the opportunity, "you can find people on the internet, if you spend some time on it."

I felt weak as dishwater watching them. So the woman, Lucille, hadn't told her husband this was their son showing up, not beforehand, not before she'd laid her eyes on James. What if he'd looked like a stranger instead?—but there was no point in going down that road.

"Should we call the kids?" the man asked.

"Owen, no, not just yet." She put a hand on his arm, as if restraining him. "I think we should ask James about his feelings on that matter. He must know we had other children. Perhaps he is angry. Are you, James? Angry at us?"

The man waved that away. "Lu, he came and found us, didn't he? That answers that." He turned to James. "Am I right?"

"Right," James answered. "That was a long time ago and everything."

Lucille ran a hand over her cheek, then pressed her temple with two fingers. "We were young," she said. "Those were hard times."

Owen stood, his hands shaking a little. "I want to show him the family albums; when he sees me and my brothers, back in the old days, he's going to think he's looking at pictures of himself."

After her husband had wiped his mouth, got up from the table and motioned for James to follow him, Lucille said to him, in a low voice, "Tell me one thing: was she good to you? Did you have a good life?"

James rose. "Sure, she was," he said. "Norma was a businesswoman, and she had a brother who came around a lot, teaching me stuff like how to catch a ball, you know."

"Yes." Lucille closed her eyes briefly and I could see the vein in her temple.

The two men sat side by side on the sofa in the living room, a stack of photo albums in front of them on the coffee table. Every single *Maarten* in America must have been kin to Owen and must have had his picture made throwing horseshoes, playing touch football, the older men playing cribbage and dominoes, the younger ones in driveways shooting baskets or on the slopes skiing. There were occasional holiday shots of wives and baby Maartens.

Owen said, "We told the kids, that's Brian and Kara, we told them from the start that we lost a baby before they came along. I don't see the problem in telling them that we found him again, the truth of the way it happened. In a nutshell, at least." He motioned for Lucille to sit, and she took my hand and led us to a pair of arm chairs facing the sofa.

Owen went on, "We'll get them back here—Brian's outside Boston with his family, and Kara, she's the one not married yet, is working on a nursing degree in Worcester. Neither one took to teaching the way we did. We'll get them here when the time is good for everybody and have a big reunion. And next year, I promise you, we'll do it up right. We'll celebrate your birthday in a proper way." And Owen Maarten gave James, his eldest son, a cuff on the shoulder, and then hooked an arm around his neck.

I considered that it might not be just me who would have certain feelings about the prodigal son's return. I wondered how Brian, who'd been the good son all along, and who probably looked like Lucille's side of the family and so not at all like a Maarten, would take the news of his new brother. And if Kara, the daughter, who hadn't rushed to marry, perhaps because of the six photo albums showing grandfathers and uncles and brothers and nephews and boy cousins and grandsons, might refuse to meet another male Maarten. Mostly, I wondered how Lucille—whose control I couldn't help but admire—felt in her heart about having her decision of twenty-eight years ago walk through her door on a Saturday in May.

James, sitting next to his dad, beaming and dazed, looked as if he'd just come downstairs on Christmas morning. As if he'd just discovered there really was a Santa Claus. I had to look away to get my mind around it. Here I'd been aching for him to have a family of his own, not realizing that once he did, he might never look back. I could have gotten in the car and headed home. He'd never have noticed.

Home

38

FROM THE FIRST day back in Peachland, it was like I'd never left. I imagined things would be different, that I'd start over fresh, but I should've known better. I'd rented a nice rose-painted bungalow with a front porch big enough for a swing, a blue bedroom upstairs where I could watch the papergirl deliver the *News* and, with the windows open, listen to the pond frogs and the phoebes. And a big fenced back yard.

That morning, I decided to walk to the pharmacy, to get dear dog used to the new town, and maybe stop for a cup of coffee, like old times, at the diner called Peanuts. I'd just turned onto the front sidewalk, walking leash in hand, when a car pulled up at the curb. Right while I watched, out stepped a girl in shorts with a baby tucked in a sling on her chest—Millie Prentice nee Dawson, who, I could see, like everyone else in town, already knew where I lived.

"Hello, Janey," she said, looking up at me, uneasy but using a friendly tone. "We—I heard you were back. Don't you look nice."

I had to give her credit. My folks and her folks and Curtis's folks along with everybody else in town would be waiting to glimpse us bumping into each other at the market pushing grocery carts, or catch us sitting across the same aisle listening to the pastor's sermon on sin and forgiveness at First

Methodist, or, sooner or later, happen on us meeting face to face at the pharmacy. The truth was, even with my heart still bruised on her account, I had to figure I owed her a favor and couldn't muster much rancor. "Hi, Millie," I returned the greeting. "I kept up with your news, since my mom says your mom shows her forty pictures of the baby every time they get together." I said it in a light way. "Congratulations."

"Thanks," she said, her face sweating. "I kept up with you, too, like you say, through our moms. And Mr. Sturgis, when I had to go in there with Danny. Babies have a lot of trouble the first year."

"They do," I agreed.

She sucked in her breath, the way she used to in grade school, when she was trying to guess the right answer. "I hope you won't mind, now, if I have to bring him in when he's sick?"

Her legs looked a little swollen still, from carrying such a load. "Millie I'm not going to not do my job, help him out with earaches and bad coughs and diaper rash, just because you and I both wasted a whole lot of our lives on Curtis Prentice. You know me well enough."

"I guess, sure," she said, looking like she'd done what she came to do and didn't know if she ought to get back in the car.

I could feel the sun beating down at nine in the morning, and worried that the tongue of my trusty transplanted companion would be on the ground by mid-afternoon in this heat. Fanning myself, to show it was nothing personal, I moved us into the shade of an old pecan tree whose roots buckled the sidewalk.

"I didn't know you were a dog person," Millie said. "You didn't used to be."

"I am," I said. "I am a dog person." Looking down at the sling across the chest that used to wear a cheerleader sweater, I smiled. "You didn't used to be a baby person, either."

She sighed but smiled also. "You learn when you have to."

"You do," I agreed.

"Your dog's got a nice disposition." She hesitated. "Maybe sometime you could bring it around for Danny to play with. What's its name?"

"Edgar," I told her. "His name is Edgar."

39

WHEN I PUT on my white coat again, it felt like I'd truly come back. Everything familiar, old times, me working where I belonged. "Good morning, *Orville*," I called to Mr. Sturgis, like we'd always been on a first-name basis.

"Janey's back!" he hollered out, giving me a big walrus-type hug around the middle, his bald head reaching my chin, and then introducing me to the new pair of Pharmacist's Assistants. And it made me feel good to see black faces again as a matter of course. "Come along, come along to the back," he said, "you won't believe the improvements." Mostly he meant new computers. "We were losing them right and left before," he told me. "Not any more."

"Patients?"

"Doctors. They said we got mired down, they said we were still puddle-jumpers in an age of jets. They must've read that in some doctors' newsletter telling them to blame things on the pharmacists. Especially, we got grief from the ones, you will recall certain well-known examples, who forget what they give a person and then go and give him something else."

That very first morning on my old job, most everybody in town came by to reassure themselves that Janey Daniels really had come back. Mr. Grady came in, the first customer, to tell me that now that Bayless was gone, he'd got himself a replacement doctor, that she made him turn in his old pills to her before he could get a new prescription, so he'd stopped getting himself into trouble. Then Mr. Haynes showed up with Blind Dog, and I thanked him for telling me about the Companion Dogs and for being a good example for me. While Edgar sniffed and rubbed noses with the large black lab, I let Mr. Haynes know how proud I'd been that my Big Dog had made it, even though losing her had been sort of like having my arms and legs ripped off, and he understood about that. I asked him for the name of a veterinarian, so I could put Edgar's windpipe in good hands, and invited him to bring Blind Dog over for a playdate soon in our new fenced yard.

Madge, Mom's friend from the bank, came in, to make sure it really was me she'd seen talking to *a certain person* in front of my pink rental this morning. And to mention that her husband Cletus, who was also my lawyer, had said anytime I wanted to tie up the ends of my settlement, just give him a call.

I turned around to greet a frail woman in a wheelchair, who had been waiting her turn, and it took me a full two minutes to recognize her as old Mrs. Runyan, the mother of the man who owned my daddy's hardware store. Her body had given out in recent months, but not her manners, and she welcomed me home with a warm, talcum-powder hug, before asking me to check, would I mind, that she was taking the right dosage.

About then, I spotted Curtis. Curtis dressed up in a tie, spit-clean and hair-combed, looking around as if he'd just that minute caught sight of me. Instead of that, I felt sure, he'd been standing around half the morning noticing who was coming in and going out. "Look who's here," he said, sauntering in the direction of the counter where I stood. "Millie says to me, 'Guess who I happened to run into today.'"

"We had a visit."

"What'd you think of my boy?"

"Oh, was that baby yours?" I gave him a pleasant look. "Since you're here, I won't have to make a phone call to remind you I'll be needing my half of the value of the house by the middle of July, don't forget."

He wrinkled his forehead as if hearing something new. Giving me time to observe he'd fleshed out his jowls along with his responsibilities. "Now, Janey," he complained, "we need to sit down and negotiate. Millie and me, we put a lot into that place, it wasn't in such good shape back when."

I took a breath and reminded myself we were standing on my turf using up my time. "You want, we can talk about it again with Cletus in his office. I need to tend to my customers."

"Hell, Janey, you haven't changed a bit."

"I'll take that as a compliment."

Then after a couple of hours, just as I was taking off my white coat to slip out for lunch, the way I used to do, late, who but Ralph Smalley should walk in. He asked had I heard the news concerning his recent divorce, if that happened to be of interest to me. I said how about let's go eat at Southern Fried, I'd been missing the food. And we did.

He looked good, a former All State player, who'd put on a loaf-of-bread size bulge at his middle and was showing a little wear and tear, but he still had the moves, striding with that spring up onto the balls of his feet that he'd perfected on the court. Walking the three blocks to the café, I figured everybody in town was watching us, drawing the same conclusion: that we'd end up together. After all, we'd gone around in high school, we'd both played pretty good basketball, we looked a pair—both a head taller than the average. And, sad if you thought about it, both of us divorced at our age. The frightening thing was wondering if I would have been thinking the same thing, strolling down the streets of Peachland with him—if I hadn't gone away? Would I have gravitated toward him out of familiarity, figuring that we more or less belonged together and might as well pick up where we left off, the way Millie and Curtis had? It gave me cold chills even to have that thought.

Over fried okra, hushpuppies, and fried catfish with a side of sweet-potato fries, he and I covered the two decades we'd shared since his folks moved here from Charleston in first grade. We talked about getting our growth early, and then about high school, when we no longer felt like freaks. When we might even have been considered cute. He admitted he'd got to be hot for a while, junior and senior year, when girls who wouldn't look at him twice before, looked at him at least once, and he went out with a few. "Including you, if my memory serves."

We talked about all the people we'd lost track of and all the people who'd had bad things happen, and who of our crowd already had four kids, and who still hadn't got married. We mentioned our moms and daddies, and the moms and daddies of all the other people we knew. And I began to feel the effects of the southern sun on my brain, wondering if anyone in this town ever did anything but talk about everybody else, from morning till night.

When we'd got our sugar-dusted fried peach turnovers and a refill on the coffee from Maydelle the owner, Ralph slid his arm over on the back of my chair—checking to make sure he wasn't disturbing the dog resting under the table. "If you'd gone to the All Night Party with me, Janey," he said, "instead of going with Curtis Prentice who you hardly knew, the rest would've been history."

"Oh, Ralph," I told him, "the rest *is* history."

40

I WAITED AT the Greenville airport for the long-lost son. For
James Maarten, who had been abroad, and come home. But I
didn't know exactly what that meant to him now, *home*.
Would he catch up with what he missed, hanging out at
Lucille and Owen's house, see about some graduate courses at
Dartmouth, it wasn't too late. On the other hand, I didn't
exactly know what it meant for me either, *home*. Was I there?
Was this it? The rose-colored cottage, the fenced yard for
Second Dog, the occasional evenings with Ralph Smalley.
Mom checking in with me every morning on the phone, catch-
ing me at the pharmacy if she didn't catch me at my rented
house, saying how the whole town was glad I had made up
with Millie.

The truth was, I missed James deep in the pit of my stomach and not a week had gone by since I got here that I didn't
think about putting Edgar in the car and heading up the highway toward the Canadian border. But my fear was: *real life
wasn't a sabbatical*. In real life, Pete, James's sidekick with the
overbite and faint acne scars and eager smile, would be all
grown up with a wife he'd met in Germany, and they'd come
eat with us on the weekend, and James might miss him hanging out with him worse than he'd missed me. Maybe I'd see
my old scroungy upstairs neighbors, Larry and Roland, at the

Pharmacy where I'd got a job in, say, South Burlington, coming in for drugs of a milder, prescriptive nature. But they too would have their own places, their pieces of paper that entitled them to decent jobs, and would scarcely recognize me in my white coat without my doggy companion. Maybe I'd stay at PACIFIC VIEW, monthly rates, while I pretended to look for a house, taking Edgar for after-work walks along the lake in the Dog Park so he could trot in the brisk air and snap at snowflakes, or to visit his former person Sylvia when she needed cheering. And we'd both be grateful not to have to spend another panting summer in muggy Carolina.

Could I do that? Leave?

He didn't look the same. Coming through the gate into the waiting area in black t-shirt, khaki pants, clean shaven, a carryon in one hand, the other slinging a jacket over his shoulder. James. *James?* I could see in my mind the straggly face-hair and grubby headband knotted around his forehead that he'd worn that first time. But here he was, all cleaned up, looking like a teacher just back from abroad. I got a lump in my throat. I didn't want improvement; I didn't want change. I wanted what I'd fallen for way back when.

"Hey," he said, his blue eyes looking happy to see me, leaning over to miss my mouth by half an inch.

"Hi," I said, slipping an arm around his neck and doing a better job of managing a welcome kiss.

"How big he is," he said, bending down to pat Second Dog.

"He is. I found him a vet, and a big yard."

He slipped the arm clutching his jacket around my shoulder. "You doing okay? About losing her?"

In the car, driving us back to Peachland, I tried to talk about my *fine good dog* which I hadn't done long distance. We'd mostly emailed during the summer, because of the time difference when he was in The Netherlands, and I'd been glad every time to see his name and read his e-talk, but it wasn't the same. His actual voice told a lot he didn't put into words.

I said, "You were right, you know, about the hydro-electric plant. That turned out to be a big step for her. Her leading me out of there."

"She did great, I told you."

"She did, but I didn't really understand, not till I saw her at the trials, backing her person away from the big scary danger—that *stupid black umbrella*." I had to pinch my nose to stop the tears. It didn't do to think about all that, and I still couldn't say her name, even to myself. Sometimes I'd think Good Big Dog, but that was all I could manage. Maybe in a year or two. I'd stuck the photos of her in the back of a Physician's Desk Reference Manual five years out of date. Maybe in a year or a dozen I could look at them.

We went up the steps of my rosy rental and he started toward the door, but I said, "Let's try out the porch swing first."

We did, pushing lightly with our feet, then I asked the real question. "How are Lucille and Owen?"

"I talked to them, but I haven't been to see them. I wanted to come down here first. But listen, I want us to take my dad over there to The Netherlands next time, see Maastricht, the town where the kids study. I want him, you know, to see his people, where they come from. I mean, I've made that trip a dozen times, and he's not even been out of the country. It's another world over there, like a century ago in a way, everybody on bicycles or on foot; going over those cobblestone bridges you hear a dozen different languages at once."

Want *us* to take him? Pete? His students? Me?

James said, "He asked how you were doing."

"How am I *doing*? I wash my undies and it's all over town before breakfast. The first day I step out my front door, my ex's wife shows up like the Welcome Wagon."

"You need to come back." He turned my face to him. "I told him, my dad, I said, Janey'll be there with me, at the reunion. That's September."

"Reunions are just for family."

"We can remedy that. Come on back."

"James, how can I leave here? Everybody in town needs me."

"You stay, you'll be double-dating with that guy you used to be married to, by Christmas." He glowered in my direction.

I nodded at the not unlikely thought. "There've been recorded cases."

"Come on, you liked Vermont." His voice rose, "You liked *me*."

I took his hand and let the swing slow to a stop. "Right on both counts."

"How about you show me your bedroom that I came all the way down here to see, now that you've really got one." He stood and hefted his bag.

"I may not be able to, you know—in this place."

"Hey, we're here, Janey. Don't get cold feet."

I smiled and opened the door—no need to lock it around here. "Not in this climate."

I let Edgar out into the green backyard, loose and off his leash since he was an ordinary dog, with a bowl of fresh water under the shady cottonwood tree.

Upstairs, out of his black t-shirt and good trousers, his heart pounding, James became his old self again, that boy I'd met at the Dog Park. Glad to have him here, I slipped out of my flowered southern dress and best new pale blue undies, and, under the breeze from the ceiling fan, we made Carolina-moon love in broad daylight on my big bed with the crisp white sheets.

He seemed agreeable—after we'd got caught up over chicken-salad sandwiches in my sunny dining room with the ceiling

fan, sharing the leftovers with Edgar, and then had a little tour
of the town in the car, so as not to attract too much attention—to the idea of meeting my parents at the Southern Fried
Café for supper. In fact, he seemed extra glad at the prospect
of seeing my daddy again, Daddy not being one for writing
thank-you letters about Sulzer Escher Wyss turbine photos.

Probably, if I hadn't been so needy to see him, so happy
he'd invited himself down, I'd have thought through what our
meeting my folks for a family supper in Peachland, South
Carolina, meant. It meant the whole town had to show up for
a look.

It was still daylight when we walked through the door, me
in a long pink skirt and tee, James in a blue shirt and khakis,
with Mom and Daddy following behind us. Daddy, nervous in
his best summer church jacket and tie, Mom in a green-and-
white flowered silk, her eyes stuck wide open with mascara.
Both of them dressed for a major public social event. The
arrival of Janey's new beau.

"This table good for you?"' Maydelle asked, lifting off the
RESERVED card next to the little vase of cut flowers.

"It's fine," I said. "Maydelle, this is my friend James
Maarten."

At once, he stuck out his hand, "Maydelle," he repeated.

While Daddy and my mom got themselves settled at the
table, deciding who should sit where, I bit the bullet and, with
James holding my hand, made the rounds of the crowded
room.

Saying hello first to Millie and Curtis, who no doubt were
sitting at the exact same table where they had eaten with her
parents in another life.

"Millie, Curtis," James repeated, hand out, eyeing my ex,
a former stud grown slack, who grudgingly offered to shake.

I greeted Madge from the bank, and her husband Cletus,
my lawyer. "This is James," I presented him.

"Madge, Cletus." He pumped their hands.

"Evening, Mr. Grady," I said, seeing he had a RESERVED card on his table also. "And, my, this must be Gloriana, all grown up. James, this is Cornelius Grady and his niece. And this is Mr. Solomon Haynes and Blind Dog, who—." I choked up and had to look away.

"Glad to meet you," James said, shaking every hand. "Good boy," he said, gently patting the big black lab.

Then he shook hands with Mr. Sturgis, who stood to his full rotund height and told him, in a near-deafening voice, how glad they were to have me back and not one instant too soon, and for him, James, not to be taking me away again any moment, now. "You hear me?"

"Mr. Sturgis," James said, "Janey talked about you all the time, and that's the truth."

"That right?" Mr. Sturgis, now *Orville* to me, looked around the room to be sure everyone caught that.

Mom had turned petunia pink with all the fuss over her only daughter having a decent looking man to show around. After we sat and gave our orders to Maydelle for the fried chicken and chicken-fried steak, fried okra and sweet-potato fries, and the buttermilk biscuits and the cornbread, deciding that we'd think about dessert later, Mom said, "We figured you for a keeper, James, we did, right from the start."

"That's right," Daddy agreed, "we figured that up there Christmas, at the home of the aunt and her *lady friend*." He said this offhand, as if his mind had already fit the two women into it and moved on.

Mom, waving at Madge, didn't appear to hear the reference to her blood kin in another sate.

After a pause, Daddy asked, "How you been, boy? I set a lot of store by that picture of the turbine you sent me. I got it mounted in the hardware."

"I gave *my* dad one, too," James said, lighting up. "He's a high school physics teacher."

"You don't say? Your dad? Huh." Daddy looked at me to see if he'd get in trouble asking a personal question outright. "Where's he at?"

"New Hampshire. My parents live in New Hampshire." James looked at the ceiling, as if amazed to hear himself say the words.

"I don't know about physics, but we've got plenty of engineering around here these days. You ought to detour over to Camden to check those little Chinese refrigerators they're turning out."

Mom looked thrilled enough to pop, and kept glancing around to note who all else in town had decided to come have supper on the spur of the moment, mid-week, at Southern Fried, and so was seeing her at the center of the event.

After a pause, Daddy asked, "You aiming to take Janey back up there, son?"

"I'm trying," James told him. "It's up to her."

I looked at the two of them, touched at the way they'd bonded. Moved that they wanted me happy and mated, that they thought the choice was mine to make. But was it? Could you ever leave if the matter of leaving rested with you? Here James had got himself a new family and a new self that he'd never imagined before. And my Good Big Dog had done the same, done her best and done it right, and moved on to her new life and new person. Could I make that happen, too? Or was I stuck here till my hair turned white as my lab coat, still making my buttermilk pie and never seeing a face I didn't already know?

"Opportunities go by," Daddy said, looking at James but maybe talking to himself or me.

"I know it, sir. They do."

I smiled at them both. "I guess I will be heading north again one of these days. I can't ask Edgar to spend another summer in this heat. And since I'll be coming up anyway at the end of August to see my Good Dog graduate with her new person, that seems as good a time as any to check out available jobs."

"You mean it?" James asked, beaming at me, giving my dad a thumbs-up.

"Would I miss your very first family reunion?"

Companion Dog

41

I HADN'T CRIED all the way from Carolina to Vermont. I didn't even cry all the way to Massachusetts from Burlington where I was staying with James. But once I drove into the parking field where I'd last been for the puppy trials, I had to blot my eyes, my face, my shirt, with half a box of Kleenex. Had to mop my eyes until even my hair felt damp.

Once I'd got myself together, I started for the section where the former persons of Companion Dogs could wait, and then, spotting Vijay's guy, himself red-faced in a stiff white dress shirt which looked right out of the box, began to weep again. He waved me over, seeming glad to see me, and blew his nose when I sat down.

"She graduating this morning?"

"I'm so proud," I sniffed.

"Yeah, I know what you mean. You take that dog that had the lung trouble?"

"I did. Edgar. He's glad to be back up here. How about you?

"It takes about two years." He blew his nose again, and pounded a fist on his thigh. "To get over them. Then, I guess, I'll start to give a thought to getting another. Vijay, he was special. But he's my third. After while you get over it and you want to try another."

"Oh, Vic. However could you go through this again?"

Then we saw the trainers turn and give a signal, and ten Companions and their persons came single file out onto the field. The graduates, the blind people, each had a chair for the ceremony, with room for their dog beside them. And there was a loudspeaker and an official photographer and a number of people I didn't recognize but who seemed, from the excitement and the way they were dressed up and waving, to be the kin of those officially getting their dogs today.

Betty had told me about Good Dog's new person. I guess all of the raisers seated, as Vic and I were, far back in sort of makeshift bleachers, close enough that we could see, but far enough away that we would not distract the dogs, had been given information. The blind woman gaining my former puppy was a sixty-five year old widow who had never wanted a dog. She didn't consider that she got on well with dogs. She'd explained that as a girl in Needham when she'd visit her uncle and his spaniel with her mother, her skirt would be covered with dog hair when she left. She didn't like the idea of moving an animal in her home; she thought of them as doing better out-of-doors. But her stepson and his wife coaxed her and cajoled her to consider the idea, telling her that she would be able to go to church again, to see her friends, to attend concerts, since they knew she quite loved chamber music. And because she, her name was Edith, was a kindly woman who realized that they'd otherwise be saddled with her care, she gave in. Allowing herself to be taken for the lengthy and intensive training sessions at the kennels. And had quite fallen in love with her gentle puppy. "They were a match from the start," Betty had said.

Trying not to break down, I watched the graduates coming along single file, and then I saw—*Beulah*. Such a big, grown-up dog, so attentive to her person, so carefully and confidently directing her to a chair. And her person: a lovely, composed older woman whose face wore a look of almost unbearable happiness: *She had done it; she had finished the course. She and her dog had many sociable and affectionate years ahead.*

"You okay?" Vic asked, standing to take a zoom photo of Vijay and the straight-backed graying man at his side.

"I'm fine," I said. "I'm really fine." And because I couldn't see too well, I handed him my camera to take a picture of the kindly lady from Needham and her Companion. In case I might want to look at it some day.